BOOK CLUB MURDER

A BOOKISH SLEUTH, A LOCKED-ROOM MURDER, AND A MYSTERY STRAIGHT OUT OF AN AGATHA CHRISTIE NOVEL

MAPLEWOOD MYSTERIES
BOOK 1

KATHLEEN GUIRE

CHAPTER 1
THE BOOK CLUB

"A MURDER IS ANNOUNCED."

I placed the last letter on the Letter board. A "d." I stepped back and admired my work.

Then, as I always do, I second-guessed my decision. It read as if I were the one announcing a murder on a letter board in the library. I reached up to pull the letters down. Too late. The familiar chime of the door let me know the first book club members had arrived. I pressed the "d" back on the board and turned to greet them.

Once everyone had filed in, balancing coffee cups and plates stacked with cookies, they settled into the half circle of chairs I'd arranged in the middle of the library. I'd tried to make it feel inviting—conversation-friendly, maybe even charming—but now it looked like we were staging an intervention. I stepped behind the cafe table I'd turned into a makeshift podium. The hum of conversation buzzed with excitement—nothing got this group going like a murder.

I flipped open the book and pushed up my glasses. James Hatterson, local bestselling mystery author and celebrity, cleared his throat before giving me a reassuring grin.

"Shall we begin?"

"Ahh, yes," I began as Agatha, my golden doodle, sniffed at the feet of Cora, another book club member. As I motioned with one of my hands to shoo her away, the copy of *A Murder is Announced* by Agatha Christie slipped—just like my dog Agatha does when she spots the first squirrel of spring and bolts, leash and all.

The antique copy of *A Murder Is Announced* hit the floor. It landed with the kind of drama that an ad in the Gazette had caused in Chipping Cleghorn—except this time, the mystery was whether I'd survive Bea Smythe's glare. The dust jacket fluttered down beside it.

I froze. Mouth open. Brain empty.

Across the room, Bea Smythe rose. Slowly. Silently. Like a librarian ghost summoned by the violation of the Dewey Decimal Code.

"That's a 1950 first edition," she said, her voice crisp enough to snap kindling. "Original dust jacket."

My cheeks burned. "I'm so sorry. It just…slipped."

She reached down before I could, her gloved hand more precise than a museum curator's. She lifted the dust jacket and gave it a once-over.

"No one ever *means* to," she murmured. "That's why we respect the books."

I nodded, lips pressed tight. I didn't dare breathe.

Then, she handed the book back, not unkindly, just… reverently. Like she was offering me one more chance to prove I belonged here. I cradled it.

Janet Kessler always smelled faintly of cinnamon and lavender furniture polish. In her early sixties, she was a retired reading specialist known for keeping to herself—unless you needed advice, a prayer, or something sweet from her ever-revolving stash of recipes. When she wasn't arranging flowers or organizing bake sales at the church, she was baking in the fellowship hall kitchen like it was sacred ground.

She had a quiet way of knowing what people needed—often before they did—and a habit of tucking handwritten recipes into her cardigan pockets like secrets.

So when Bea puffed up like a threatened rooster over the dropped book, Janet didn't even blink.

"Oh, Bea," she said, brushing a bit of flour off her skirt. "Don't get so worked up. That book was just sitting on a shelf in my guest room. That's why I donated it. I want it to be used. Loved. Not kept like a museum piece."

She passed me a napkin with a warm white chocolate and cranberry cookie. "Besides, Miss Marple's tougher than she looks."

Bea sat, smoothed her skirt, and folded her hands. "Well," she said, her voice settling like a gavel. "Shall we see who's been murdered?"

The book club had recently finished one of James's books and although they loved it, I felt we should consider other authors. Who was I kidding? Agatha Christie was my favorite. I named my dog after her. My coping mechanism was quoting Miss Marple. At least twice a year, I suggested an Agatha Christie novel.

"It's okay, Gabby." Cora motioned to Agatha, who

was busy licking her expensive, sharp-toed stiletto boots. "I must have dropped some of my salmon wrap on them."

I recovered my book and my composure. "Before we get started, Antonio, did you take attendance?"

"Yes, we have a lot of people here today," he reported instead of giving me an actual number.

No wonder it felt so stuffy. Often it was my retirees and me, The Sleuths they called themselves. They met every day here in the library at nine a.m. and discussed everything from books to politics. Last winter they'd helped me solve the murder of Councilman Bernard Cass when my best friend Brittany had been accused.

"Let's start with the advertisement in the paper," James suggested as I eyed the snacks, wondering if I'd set out enough.

"Yes, would someone like to read it?"

Time to harness my thoughts and pay attention. The book club had been my idea — a way to bring more of the community into the library when the Kindle and other reader apps were giving us some stiff competition.

As head librarian, not only was my job at stake if I didn't keep people coming, but the community suffered. The library should be a hub offering a chance not only for education but for connection.

Cora adjusted the stack of neatly labeled discussion notes in her lap, her perfectly lined blazer not quite hiding the exhaustion in her eyes. She was the kind of woman who color-coded her planner and still found time to make homemade candles for everyone in the group. Book club was her one true escape, and she treated it with the reverence of a holiday dinner she didn't have to cook.

"Before we start." Cora stood. Cora, ever prepared, opened her leather satchel and began handing out candles, each one labeled in her careful script like a tiny, scented thank-you note. Agatha took this as a signal to help her. She trotted over and poked her nose into the satchel.

"I made these for everyone. I tried to get your favorite fragrance."

Janet stood to help her. "Tell me who gets what, sweetie. What a thoughtful gift."

"Ummm. James." As she said his name, she blushed. "Spice."

Many members of the community acted like a blushing schoolgirl in the presence of James.

He stood, straightened his suit lapel and took a bow. "Oh my dear, so nice of you to think of me."

"Antonio gets the basil."

Janet took the sage green candle and handed it to him. Antonio owned Tony's Pizza. His grandson ran it now. I wasn't sure why he needed a candle that smelled like the very herb that emanated from his clothes and skin. As if he had bathed in it for the last forty years.

For the next ten minutes, Cora handed out candles. Some book club members took this opportunity to grab a second cup of coffee from the fancy machine in what we called the fishbowl room, a soundproof glass room in the middle of the library.

"Ruthie, I made this lemon-verbena candle just for you."

I didn't hear Ruthie's response, because I joined the

other coffee drinkers. James took over the machine and pressed a shot of espresso for me. The machine was his gift to the library. He'd typed his first bestseller here at the Maplewood Library on a typewriter.

I couldn't hear the response, but I knew Ruthie would say kind words in a derogatory tone that let everyone know she was better than them. Scratch that. She would say kind words with a plastic smile.

As I sipped the tiny espresso James handed me, Cora stuck her head in the door. "Gabby, I have a candle for you."

She stepped into the room and thrust a psychedelic candle at me with every color of the rainbow swirled in. "Like your pants," she explained.

I looked down at my pastel-colored plaid pants. I'd picked them up at Second Time Chic last week. I set my espresso cup down and took the candle in both hands.

"It's absolutely perfect, Cora. I love it."

She grinned. "I'm so glad you like it. I added a lavender scent to help you with your anxiety."

Instead of shutting down or making a smart quip, I laughed out loud. Another anxiety-ridden, do-you-really-like-me? reaction.

"I think we should get started. Thank you, Cora for making everyone candles." I exited the fishbowl room and took my seat in the circle, after setting the candle down on the table with six others.

Instead of James clearing his throat again to get everyone's attention, Thomas, another one of The Sleuths, began reading. Thomas had the kind of voice everyone listened to with rapt attention. As a retired councilman and real estate agent, he'd had plenty of practice.

He stood and paced. "The advertisement reads:

'A murder is announced and will take place on Friday, October 29, at Little Paddocks, at 6:30 p.m. Friends, please accept this, the only intimation.'" [1]

"Someone announced a murder in the newspaper?" Antonio exclaimed as he thumbed through the book. "Where is that?"

"Thank you for announcing you haven't read the chapters," James replied.

Antonio wasn't deterred by the comment. "It says it more than once." He pointed to another quote of the advertisement.

"Yes, Agatha is introducing all the characters in a foreshadowing. It gives the reader a glimpse of how each player responds to the ad," I suggested.

"The dog wrote this book?" Antonio scanned Agatha, his gaze fixing on her wagging tail.

"And this is exactly why I don't come to book club." Ruthie set her book on her lap and crossed her arms.

Antonio ignored her and went back to the book. Everyone ignored Ruthie's comment and began to thumb through the book and count the number of times the ad showed up.

"Should we bring out the board?" Randolph, the retired county coroner suggested.

Ruthie huffed and examined her perfectly manicured nails. "It's not like we are solving a real murder."

As James and Randolph stood to wheel our murder board out of the back hallway, I wondered why Ruthie had come. She came intermittently. Usually once a quarter. Most of the time, she didn't know what we were reading, choosing to grab a copy of our current read from the library shelves. She dressed in thousand-dollar pantsuits and entered in a cloud of expensive perfume. She never had a hair out of place.

I didn't have time to pursue the why-is-Ruthie-here line of thought. James and Randolph wheeled the board out. Thomas joined them at the board and wielded a dry-erase marker. Janet and Cora stood and shouted out the names of characters.

Antonio stood and raised his copy of *A Murder Is Announced* in the air like a flag. "I counted three times the ad is read."

"Antonio, hold that thought." Thomas held the book open and copied:

'A murder is announced and will take place on Friday, October 29, at Little Paddocks, at 6:30 p.m. Friends, please accept this, the only intimation.'" [2]

Randolph capped the marker and chose a different color. "Now the number of times it was read, Antonio."

"I count three so far," Antonio reported.

Randolph stood at the whiteboard, uncapped marker in hand. "Okay, let's list out the suspects from *A Murder Is Announced*. Who's first?"

Simone waved her hand like we were in a classroom. "Letty Blacklock! She owns Little Paddocks where it all goes down."

"Right." Randolph scrawled *Letitia Blacklock* in bold letters at the top. "Next?"

Janet, already halfway through her second cranberry and white chocolate cookie, said, "Bunny. Dora Bunner. Poor thing—so chatty, so doomed."

"Got it." He wrote *Bunny* and underlined it.

Cora leaned forward. "Phillipa Haymes. She's the quiet widow—always a red flag in Christie's books."

"Ooooh, yes," Bea chimed in. "And Mitzi! You can't forget her. The housekeeper who thinks everyone's trying to poison her."

Randolph laughed as he jotted *Mitzi – housekeeper (dramatic!)* next to Phillipa's name.

Simone sipped her coffee and added, "Inspector Craddock. Sharp guy. Miss Jane Marple collaborates with him."

"Craddock," Randolph repeated, adding him under *Investigators*. "And Miss Marple, of course. Our queen."

"Colonel Easterbrook!" Janet said with enthusiasm. "The blustery old colonel—suspicious of everyone."

Cora nodded. "And his wife, Laura. So glamorous and completely uninterested in his theories."

"Miss Hinchcliffe and Miss Murgatroyd," Bea added quickly. "They were such close companions. Loved their banter."

Randolph tapped the board with his marker. "Okay, this is getting full. Anyone else?"

Simone raised her eyebrows. "Don't forget Edmund Swettenham—the snarky young writer—and his doting mother, Mrs. Swettenham. She was always fussing over him."

As Randolph added their names to the list, Agatha took advantage of the distraction to nose her way under the snack table, emerging triumphantly with a napkin full of cookie crumbs stuck to her muzzle.

"Agatha," I hissed, trying to look authoritative

while wiping her face with the edge of my sleeve. "You are not part of the refreshments."

A round of laughter bubbled through the room.

"Honestly," I muttered as I straightened up. "It's a miracle we ever get through a chapter with you all." But I was smiling—and so was everyone else. The hum of conversation buzzed again, energized by sugar, caffeine, and murder.

Oh! And what about Pip and Emma?" Janet asked, her eyes lighting up.

Randolph tilted his head. "Right—they're the mystery heirs, aren't they? Belle Goedler left her fortune to one of them, but their identities were hidden the whole time."

Cora nodded. "Turns out we actually *do* meet them—Phillipa is Pip, and Emma was pretending to be Julia Simmons the whole time."

"That twist got me," Bea added, shaking her head. "I didn't see it coming until the very end."

Randolph underlined their names on the board and added a star. "Worth remembering. No one does secret identities like Christie."

"True," Bea agreed. "But they caused half the trouble. Might as well write *Pip & Emma (Fake Heirs?)* and circle it in red."

He added the names with a flourish and circled them dramatically. "Red herring central."

The room buzzed with warm laughter and rustling notebooks as Randolph capped the marker. "There we have it—Chipping Cleghorn's most suspicious."

A few more regulars added their opinions as the board filled up with names.

Beatrice "Bea" Smythe, the retired librarian who I'd trained with and then replaced, stood. She pushed her glasses up her long and pointed nose and then looked over them. "Why would you announce a murder? Aren't you leaving a trail of evidence for the police to follow?"

"Exactly," I replied, glancing in her direction. Of course I'd read the entire book and I shouldn't give anything away.

She returned the glance with a steely gaze that librarians perfect after years of looking down at patrons who've had one too many overdue books. "Do tell, Gabby."

I swallowed hard before continuing and reminded myself I was head librarian now and did not have any overdue books. Did I? I shook my head slightly before continuing. "The ad is to get the neighbors to show up."

"For the murder?" Owen Gallagher, the reclusive mystery writer scribbled notes in a leather journal. Every year Owen bragged he was writing a bestseller. James Hatterson had offered to look at his work, but Owen had simply clutched his ever present leather journal to his chest. "No thanks, I've got it."

He normally spent the book club meetings scribbling notes and not offering anything to the group except an occasional "I wouldn't write it that way." Or when we finished a murder mystery, he'd say "Yeah I figured out who the murderer was in the first chapter."

After book club meetings, Owen visited the snack table and stuffed cookies and muffins wrapped in napkins in a worn leather briefcase that looked as if it had been around since 1950. He claimed it had belonged to Rex Stout, author of the Nero Wolfe Mysteries, and yet he treated it as if it were a trash can. He shoved notes into the briefcase, which was full of folders for his latest bestselling novel-in-progress. Only there never was a novel.

Simone Caldwell took over as Owen scribbled notes. "Agatha is a genius."

Agatha the dog gave a quick yip at the compliment.

"We know you didn't write the book." Antonio gave her a quick pat as she licked his shoes.

Simone continued, "Great pick, Gabby." Simone was a retired teacher with a short fuse, but only with those students who weren't the brightest lightbulb in the room, like Antonio. Of course, he was never her student. Maybe her classmate.

I'd been her student and, because she thought my lightbulb was bright, I was never on the receiving end of her smart and cutting remarks. The kind of remarks that shaped how a student felt about themselves, sometimes for the rest of their lives.

"Thank you, Mrs. Caldwell." Suddenly I felt like a student all over again. I'd often felt second-hand embarrassment for other students when they squirmed under her steely gaze.

"It's just Simone now, Gabby. You were my best student, you know."

"What is this? Book club or a popularity contest?" Ruthie complained.

My cheeks flushed hot for two reasons – I didn't take compliments well. I didn't like Ruthie disrespecting Mrs. Caldwell, and I had a sneaking suspicion

Ruthie had something to do with Mrs. Caldwell getting investigated our senior year.

"Thanks, Simone. Honestly, Miss Christie was a master of her craft. *A Murder Is Announced* is a perfect example of how effortlessly she pulls you in—setting up the crime, gathering all the suspects in one place with that seemingly harmless joke ad in the *Gazette*, and then—bam! Chaos erupts. And right from the start, she captures that small-town nosiness so well. Remember the first chapter? *'A murder is announced'* I mean, who wouldn't be hooked after that? It's classic Christie—deceptively simple, utterly brilliant."

"So, we must assume, the ad was meant to gather the characters?" Janet asked.

"I think so," James answered. "And introduce the characters. Genius. I mean my dear, who would actually advertise a murder in the ad section?"

At this point, Owen *harrumphed* and crossed something out in his notebook.

The timer on my phone buzzed. "That's all the time we have for tonight." I stood and smoothed my lilac cardigan and added, "Make sure you grab some snacks and don't forget your candle."

There was no need to tell Owen to take home leftover snacks. He was already at the table, wrapping a stack of white chocolate cranberry cookies in a napkin.

James caught my eye and smiled as he tilted his head in Owens' direction. "I tried to help the dear boy," he whispered when he got close enough. "I'll clean the coffee machine."

Others in the book club exited quickly without grabbing snacks. I'd have to pack those up later and save them for the morning meeting of The Sleuths. Right now, Agatha needed to go out and do her business. I clipped her leash on her collar and then noticed three candles left on the table. Mine and two others.

After securing Agatha, I grabbed the two others and went out the back to the parking lot. Agatha trotted across the parking lot and stopped at a running car.

Ruthie was talking on her phone in her Lexus. I tapped on the window. She rolled it down long enough to stick an arm out and grab a candle. "Oh…. yeah, she's a real witch… not you Gabby… thanks." She hit a button and the window rolled up.

"Janet," I yelled when I spotted her at the edge of the parking lot. "Your candle." I held up the candle as proof.

Agatha zipped across the remaining space between us and yipped as I jogged behind her as if to say "Keep up, Gabby."

Janet lived a block from the library so it made sense for her to walk, but after Councilman Bernard had been murdered right here in the parking lot, I didn't think she should walk alone. I caught up, gave her the candle, and asked if she'd mind some company.

"Thank you, Gabby. It's a dark night." She held up the candle. "Maybe we should light this." She added with a chuckle.

CHAPTER 2
THE CRIME

MY BEST FRIEND, Brittany, sent me a text as I was unlocking the library the next morning.

> Sorry I missed book club last night.
> Chasing down a story that didn't
> pan out

As I turned on the lights, she shot me another text.

> My mom wants to know if you liked the
> white chocolate cranberry cookies. She
> gave Janet the recipe, so she wants to
> get the credit if they were good.

I set my messenger bag down on a table so I could answer her. Of course we loved the cookies.

Sally, Brittany's mom, was the queen of baked goods. One of her famous sayings was "Baked goods make everything better." And most of the time that was true. Except for the time Brittany was arrested for murder.

I texted back:

> Yes. Everyone loved the cookies.

She responded:

> Did Owen stuff a few in that briefcase he says belonged to Rex Stout?

I responded with a quick "yes." giggling emoji

I giggled remembering Owen grabbing a napkin and wrapping a stack of cookies up, trying to be covert, but we all saw him. Not to mention, we knew his habits.

Agatha yipped to announce the library was open. She immediately loped to her giant maroon pillow and settled down for a nap.

No more texts from Brittany. I'd see her later. We had plans to meet at The Tasty Burger for lunch. Right now, I needed to get ready for the daily meeting of The Sleuths. Because it wasn't a story hour morning, I had a bit more time to set up. After retrieving the leftovers from last night's book club, I set them up in the fishbowl room. I started a regular pot of coffee. I'd let James handle the espresso shots when he came in. By that I meant he could make me a few shots.

———

Two events happened at the same time. A siren wailed up the back street beside the library — the same back street Janet and I had walked last night in the dark with only our phone flashlights to guide us. The four members of The Sleuths entered the building, evidenced not only by their chatter but the door chime.

Agatha responded by leaving her comfy pillow and running in circles, yapping and jumping like she was a circus animal performing for the crowd.

I stepped from behind the counter. "What's going on?"

"I haven't a clue, my dear," James said. "We were walking here and heard the ambulance siren."

"We were hoping you knew," Thomas said as he took his hat off and set it on a table.

The sirens cut off abruptly—not far. Too close. Somewhere behind the library, in the direction of Janet's little blue house with the ivy-covered porch

"Do you know anyone who lives in the neighborhood behind the library?" Randolph added, and then quickly corrected himself. "Of course. Janet."

"Was she sick?" Antonio asked.

I stepped back. Janet. The one who always had a kind word and warm cookies. She kept to herself, sure —but she's the one who made the library feel like a sanctuary, not just a building full of books. Fresh flowers on the desk, a quiet smile, and those afternoons when she'd bring in the kids she babysat—it was like she left a little warmth in every corner.

Just the thought of something happening to her sent a jolt through me.

The sound of the ambulance had already unsettled me, but hearing her name? That's when my trauma trigger tripped.

It always caught me off guard, even after all these

years. One moment I was standing in the library, and the next I was a little girl again, staring at red water in a white bathtub. My mother's wrists. The silence afterward. The sharp, metallic tang of blood mixed with the overpowering scent of Dial soap—orange, medicinal, and impossible to forget.

I blinked hard, trying to stay in the present. This wasn't then. This was now. And Janet—

Janet had to be okay.

"No. I walked her home last night. She was fine."

James patted me on the shoulder. "Don't jump to conclusions, dear. Your literary-mystery mind is getting the better of you."

I straightened my cardigan. "You're right. We don't know that it is Janet."

"Shall I make you an espresso?" James asked.

"I give Agatha a treat and she calmed down," Antonio bragged.

"Thank you, Antonio." Although rewarding Agatha for performing like a circus dog probably wasn't the best idea, Antonio meant well.

I turned to James. "Make it a double."

The door chimed and two library employees entered. They didn't mention the sirens, so they must have missed them. I asked Mary, my assistant, to man the library while I joined The Sleuths in the fishbowl room for coffee.

Mary plopped her large handbag on the counter. She scanned the library. "Sure, boss. Looks pretty quiet in here." True. We were the only ones here. Brad had left us to reshelve books, his preferred activity. Talking to people wasn't his strong suit.

Once in the fishbowl room, I couldn't push the quote that had been pressing upon me since I heard the sirens.

"The worst is so often true." (quote-They Do It With Mirrors)

Randolph pulled out a chair and motioned to it.

"You've had quite a shock."

Antonio scrunched his face up, his eyes disappearing in the pudge. "I don't understand." He looked outside the fishbowl. "Nothing happened."

"This is a past trauma trigger," James explained as he handed me an espresso cup. "Drink this. I added some sugar for the shock."

"You know that doesn't work." Randolph crossed his arms. "I know you use it in your novels. But in real life sugar activates anxiety. It increases cortisol levels, the body's main stress hormone."

"Gentleman, this isn't the time to argue," Thomas, always the diplomat, interjected. "Gabby is suffering."

"I still do not understand," Antonio added while wringing his large doughy hands.

I swallowed a swig of espresso. With all eyes on me, I explained, "When I was a child, I was… removed from the home… the sirens… I remember the red and blue lights…"

Antonio kneeled on the floor in front of me and took one of my hands."We don't let anyone take you again."

Instead of rising after his promise, he stayed on his knees.

"Help me up, someone. These knees, they don't work so good anymore."

I couldn't help but laugh. The other Sleuths joined me as Randolph and Thomas hefted Antonio to his feet.

James knew more of my story than the other Sleuths. He gave me a sad smile and a nod. I decided not to share any more right now.

I stood and grabbed a muffin. "Thank you Antonio. Thank you everyone. I'm sure I was overreacting." Meaning I was fine. Janet was fine. Right?

The other men joined me, raiding the snacks and pouring coffee. The conversation turned to other things. Namely, last night's book club.

James lamented he'd tried once again to help Owen write his "bestselling novel."

"Trouble is, that kid has ten ideas for novels, but no idea how to create an outline or a character."

I grabbed a second muffin.

"And yet he scribbles notes during every book club meeting and stuffs them in his briefcase."

Randolph poured himself a second cup of coffee. "And shows up for the next meeting and does the same."

"Ruthie coming was unexpected," I added, changing the subject. I felt bad for Owen, but if he wouldn't accept help, there was nothing we could do about it.

Thomas leaned forward in our circle as if he were telling us a secret. "She seems to attend once a quarter."

"Why she do that?" Antonio asked, his eyes wide with curiosity.

"Easy," Thomas said with a knowing nod. "If she ever decides to run for office, she can slap it on her record as community involvement."

I set my espresso cup down. "You think she's planning on running for office?"

Before Thomas could answer, Mary stuck her head in the fishbowl room. "There's a detective here to speak to you."

I swiveled around so quickly I lost my balance. I steadied myself on Thomas' arm. I followed Mary's gaze, and my stomach dropped—Detective Brandon stood there, flanked by two uniformed officers, their eyes locked on me.

"What's going on, Detective?" Thomas asked as he stepped out of the fishbowl.

My phone buzzed and I pulled it out of my cardigan pocket. Brittany had texted me.

Janet Kessler was found dead this morning.

I texted back quickly, knowing Detective Brandon was most probably here about her death. I'm sure I was the last person to see her, which made me a suspect if it was murder.

Was it murder?

The text whooshed, but before I could wait for an answer, Detective Brandon had entered the fishbowl room.

"Gabby, I need to talk to you."

"Janet is dead," I stated.

"How did you?… Never mind." He turned to The Sleuths. "Could I have the room?"

James refused to budge. "My dear detective, Gabby had nothing to do with Janet's death."

Brandon ignored him and pointed at the door with the two imposing officers flanking it. Of course, everyone in town knew the two imposing officers. I'd gone to school with both of them. But The Sleuths respected authority for the most part.With the clanking of coffee cups, shuffling feet, and a slow-motion snack table raid, The Sleuths headed out like a herd of turtles —bumping into each other and nearly toppling the last plate of white chocolate cranberry cookies.

"Sometime today would be good," Detective Brandon snapped.

Agatha trotted after the men as they headed out, pausing just long enough to give Detective Brandon's shoes a thorough sniff—like she was making sure he passed inspection. I reached down, scooped her up and held her to my chest for comfort. "Remember they helped you solve the last murder here in Maplewood."

Antonio was the last to leave. He held up a freshly poured cup of coffee which sloshed on the floor. Agatha rocketed forward to clean it up. As the officers took the muffins Antonio offered them, James slipped a dictionary in the doorway, propping the door open. The room was no longer sound proof. They could hear every word we said.

Detective Brandon was too busy staring at me to notice. As he glared at me, I couldn't help but give James, Thomas, Randolph, and Antonio a pleading look as they settled at the round table closest to the fishbowl door.

I echoed Thomas's earlier question. "What's this

about? Are you here because I was the last one to see Janet and you suspect me?" I planted my hands on my hips in my best *how-could-you-think-that* stance.

He ran his hands through his hair. "No... I ... can you take a seat?"

"Not until you call off the big dogs."

I knocked on the glass wall of the fishbowl room. Both officers turned, muffins in hand. I cracked the door open just enough and gave them a quick wave.

"Hey, Gabby," Officer Greg said with a grin. "These are so good. Did Brittany's mom—Sally—make them?"

I smiled. "Yes, she did."

"Remember when we used to hang out at Brittany's and watch movies? Her mom always made cookies," Officer Shane added, reaching for another muffin and stuffing the whole thing into his mouth.

"This isn't a high school reunion," Detective Brandon muttered, already moving.

With two long strides, he reached the door, spotted the dictionary James had used to prop the door open—the same one I regularly used to keep the door from locking me in—and kicked it aside. The door swung shut with a solid click. Agatha, who had been camped out just inside the doorway in hopes of scavenging crumbs, barked her protest and darted around the fishbowl room, yapping at the sealed door.

We couldn't hear her, of course.

I sat in the chair Detective Brandon offered. "Janet's death wasn't murder. I just wanted to let you know since you were friends with her." He pulled out his notebook and read. "And you walked her home from book club last night?"

"If it wasn't murder why are you taking case notes?"

I hadn't processed the fact that Janet was dead. Right now, I was wrapped up in my reaction not only to the sirens, but to the detective marching into the library with two officers. Felt like an investigation to me. Before I could squash it, a Miss Marple-like saying slipped out.

"One has to assume sometimes the most unlikely things, especially when one is dealing with murder."

"I just said it wasn't murder." He slammed a hand on the snack table and a mini muffin toppled on the floor.

I regained my composure and stood. "Then why are you here interrogating me and strong-arming me with Greg and Shane?"

Greg and Shane still guarded the door, if you could call what they were doing guarding. Shane was holding Agatha in his arms and scratching her belly. Agatha's head was leaned back in complete surrender. Greg had pulled his phone out and was texting someone. His back was toward us, but by the rise and fall of his shoulders, it appeared he was laughing.

Detective Brandon followed my gaze. Once he realized his officers weren't looking…well, *intimidating* was the word I'd guess ... he jiggled the handle. It stuck. He gave the door a sharp shove and stormed out.

I really needed to get that door fixed.

"Let's go, officers."

Agatha jumped to the floor, her free massage over. She yipped her disapproval.

Detective Brandon turned to me. "I just came to tell you your friend had died. It wasn't murder."

"How can you be sure?" Randolph asked, slipping back into his coroner role.

The detective stopped, his two officers almost knocking into him like a slapstick comedy movie.

"Because she died in a locked room." He took two more strides before turning and saying, "Our *new* coroner will handle the autopsy."

"I thought you said natural causes." Randolph stood. "Why the autopsy?"

Detective Brandon didn't answer the question. He turned to me. "Tell Brittany not to write an article about this."

"I hardly think Gabby is going to squash Brittany's freedom of the press," James offered.

Detective Brandon didn't acknowledge James's comment. He had already left the building along with Shane and Greg, who both gave apologetic waves from outside the window.

"A locked-door murder mystery," I said more to myself than anyone.

CHAPTER 3
THE PUSHBACK

THE NEXT MORNING, I poured myself a cup of coffee before retrieving the newspaper from the front porch. Agatha joined me, running out into the rain-soaked yard to do her business. My neighbor, Miranda, stepped out at the same time and gave me a quick wave. She was dressed in a silk blouse, lilac-colored power suit and full make-up. Did she wake up that way?

I waved down and pulled my ratty terry cloth robe tighter. It was ratty because when I first brought Agatha home, she claimed the bottom of it as her chew toy. She had systematically chewed on the hem all the way around until it had unraveled. I couldn't bear to part with it because Agatha loved it so much.

Miranda opened her door and immediately returned to the front porch. She waved her newspaper in a perfectly manicured hand adorned with diamonds. "Gabby, did you see Brittany's article? 'A Locked-Door

Murder.'" Before I could answer, Agatha took off through the yard and joined Miranda on her porch.

"Oh, hi, Agatha." She reached down and patted her. "Come over for a cup of coffee? I have fifteen minutes."

Without waiting for a response, she reached inside and grabbed a towel to dry Agatha off before letting her in. Agatha visited her often enough that she had a towel and treats for her.

I slipped back inside, grabbed my yellow rain boots and yanked them on. I took a quick glance in the mirror and smoothed down my copper locks. They didn't want to be smoothed down. I grabbed a hat and shoved it on my head. Great. I looked like a homeless person. Ratty robe. Plaid pajama pants. Not to mention a rain hat and boots. Oh well, here goes. I stepped out of the door and sploshed across the front yard to Miranda's.

Sixty-seconds later, I was sipping coffee in Miranda's gleaming kitchen that smelled of lemon and violets. I had left my muddy rain boots at the door. Agatha lounged on an expensive pillow on the floor as if she lived here.

"Listen to this." She read me the first paragraph of Brittany's article.

"Janet Kessler was the last person anyone expected to meet a violent end. At 70, she was a pillar of the community—volunteering at the church, organizing book drives at the library, and always ready with a kind word. Yet, on Tuesday morning, she was found dead in her locked bedroom, the door bolted from the inside, with no sign of forced entry. The question haunting Maplewood isn't just how she died—but

why? Who would want to harm a woman so beloved, and more chillingly, how did they get in—and out—without a trace?"

"What? She said it was murder?" I grabbed the rolled up paper I had in my robe pocket and smoothed it out on the table.

"What are the police saying?" Miranda asked.

I continued to scan the paper.

She stood and grabbed the coffee cup I'd drained. She placed it under the nozzle of a fancy machine and pressed a button. "I'm sorry. I thought you were dating Detective Brandon."

I swallowed hard. "Oh, we went on one date. I wouldn't exactly call it dating."

"Well, the girls at the real estate office say he stopped at the library to talk to you directly after visiting Janet's house." She set my frothy coffee brew down in front of me.

Her real estate office, Clearview Realty Group, was across the street from the library. With sweeping windows across the front of her ultra-modern building, she and her staff could observe everything on the main street.

I took a sip of the coffee and then reached for a cloth napkin to wipe my frothy mustache.

"No, he came to let me know she was dead and that it was *not* murder."

Her watch buzzed, and she gave it a quick tap before looking back at me.

"And to intimidate you," she added, like it was the most obvious thing in the world.

I blinked. "Intimidate me?"

Miranda shrugged, that knowing glint in her eye. "Men like him don't just show up in uniform and stay silent for no reason. He's keeping you on edge—seeing what you'll say when you're nervous."

I opened my mouth to argue, but...well, she *was* Miranda. She saw angles I didn't—even when I was standing right in them.

Miranda's watch buzzed for a second time.

"Do you need to go?" I asked.

"No. Just a reminder. Janet's son, Brett, wants me to look at the property and give him my opinion on how much he can get for it." She took a sip of coffee and muttered under her breath, "Vulture."

"What?"

"I mean she's not even buried and Brett is ready to sell the place. I think he's having money issues."

"Is he?" I shifted in my seat, my inner detective blinking like a giant red light. No, I wasn't investigating. This *wasn't* murder.

"Oh, sorry. My girls and I kind of see everything in this town, and we tend to love gossip." She rose and glided to the sink, placing her cup in it.

I took that as my cue to do the same.

"What else are you not telling me? About Brett?" Okay. I wasn't investigating. But I was still curious.

She turned and leaned forward as if she were whispering a secret. "Just last week, Brett came into the office and asked one of my junior agents to list his home with the excuse he was downsizing."

Her watch buzzed again. "Oh, I've got to go! Lock the door behind you?"

I glanced at my plain old-fashioned watch. "I've got to go too. The library won't open itself."

As we stepped out the front door, I turned to her. "You should come to book club."

"Oh, thank you, Gabby, but I don't go in for that bodice-ripping and romance." She fished her keys out of her purse and headed down the walk.

Her pearl-white Lexus RX sat in the driveway, spotless and parked at the perfect angle, like it belonged in a real estate brochure. She pressed the remote start button with a practiced flick, and the engine hummed quietly to life.

Agatha rushed across the sidewalk to my yard and up the porch steps. "Oh... you must have heard some misinformation. We read mysteries."

Her eyes widened. "You do?"

"Yes." Agatha yipped twice. "We're reading *A Murder Is Announced* by Agatha Christie."

"Well, I never would have guessed that. I know Cora attends and she's not the intellectual type, if you know what I mean."

I squelched across the yard to quiet Agatha.

Miranda tiptoed through her yard to her car, heels careful on the stone pavers. "Text me the info and I'll be there!"

———

My buttercup-yellow VW Bug sat under the maple tree like a daffodil parked on the curb. The paint was a little faded from too many summers, and the passenger seat bore the unmistakable signs of Agatha's reign—nose smudges on the window, a paw print or two on the dash, and one well-loved library tote she refused to give up. The car wasn't flashy, but it ran like a dream and had enough personality to hold its own against the sleek SUVs of Maplewood. Just like me. I walked in the front door of the library. Thankfully, Mary had opened.

"Thanks for opening the library," I said.

Mary looked at me, clearly puzzled. "I was on the schedule. You don't always have to be here first, boss."

One of the lessons I learned from running the library and meeting with The Sleuths was I didn't have to go it alone. But I tried going it alone most days anyway.

"Oh, and Detective Brandon and Brittany are here."

I did a quick visual sweep of the library. The fishbowl room. They had the door closed so I couldn't hear what they were saying. It was evident by Brittany's animated arms and red face that they were arguing.

"He came to talk to you." Mary leaned on the counter and watched the fishbowl show. "But she showed up and he tore into her. I suggested they take it outside."

"And Brittany said she wasn't leaving?" I suggested.

"Yep. Said Detective Brandon couldn't harass you at your place of employment."

"Let me guess. She also said 'The freedom of the press isn't just a right—it's a responsibility to seek the truth, ask the hard questions, and never look away.'"

I set my hat and coat on the counter and Mary took them.

"Can you keep Agatha here?" I asked as I pushed up my sleeves and prepared to enter the fishbowl fight.

I opened the door.

Brittany turned and saw me. "Gabby, I've been texting you all morning."

I patted my pockets. "I forgot my phone."

"And I've called you," Brandon added.

I raised an eyebrow. "Really?"

"Don't get too excited," Brittany spat. "It wasn't to ask you out on a date. It was to ask me to forgo my right as a journalist."

Brandon pointed a finger at her and shook it. "She needs to retract her article."

"And what does that have to do with me?" I asked while motioning toward the door with a cardigan-clad arm. "I have patrons coming in."

Detective Brandon stopped and did a one-eighty scan of the library. "There's no one here."

"The Sleuths are coming," Brittany shot. "And they use this room."

I was not going to mention The Sleuths. Just the mention of The Sleuths would set off another argument. But Brittany wasn't afraid of starting a debate.

True to form, she put her hands on her hips. "You're planning on solving this, aren't you?"

"How many times do I have to say this? Janet was not murdered." He picked up the jacket he'd thrown on a leather chair. "Retract that statement." He shoved his arm into his jacket sleeve. "And Gabby, don't you and The Sleuths try to solve a crime that doesn't exist."

CHAPTER 4
THE SLEUTHS

"CAN'T YOU SEE MY DEAR?" James asked as he balanced a stack of murder mysteries in one arm. With the other arm, he reached for another Agatha Christie book. "This is our chance to solve a locked-door murder."

"Are you pulling all the locked-door murder books off the shelf?" Randolph asked as he relieved James of the first stack.

"I'll take those to the table," Antonio offered and took the stack from Randolph. My library had turned into a murder mystery factory line.

"I've got the murder board," Thomas yelled in an exaggerated whisper from across the room.

Agatha ran around the table housing the locked-door murders and barked in agreement. There seemed to be nothing I could do. The Sleuths were determined to solve the non-murder simply because Janet died in a locked room.

"Why did she lock her bedroom door?" Antonio asked. "When she's home alone. It makes no sense."

"I heard her son was having money trouble. Maybe she hid her valuables in there," Thomas offered as he plunked the dry erase markers on the whiteboard ledge.

"So… maybe Brett is a suspect," James filled in as he hefted another small stack of books onto the table.

"Locked-room murder," I said aloud, almost to myself. "It has all the markings."

Randolph glanced up from behind a stack of Agatha Christie paperbacks. "You mean like *The Murders in the Rue Morgue*?" He wiggled his eyebrows. "Or am I getting my detectives mixed up?"

"Wrong author," I said, suppressing a smile. "But good instinct. Poe started the trend, Christie perfected it."

James popped his head around the board. "So you think this whole thing is staged? Like someone's reenacting a book?"

"I think," I said, tugging *Murder in the Mews* from Antonio's pile, "someone's copycatting classic locked-room mysteries. And if they're using Christie as a blueprint, we're going to need all the clues we can get."

Antonio handed me *Dead Man's Mirror*. "This one too, right? Suicide in a locked study, turns out to be murder."

"Exactly." I laid the book beside the others on the center table. "In *The Dream*, there were witnesses who swore no one entered the room before the man was found dead. Poirot had to prove the killer got in another way."

Randolph set down *Hercule Poirot's Christmas* with a theatrical sigh. "If someone murdered Janet in the spirit of holiday cheer in the first throws of spring, I'm going to need more coffee."

"She was found alone. Door locked. No sign of struggle. The perfect locked-room illusion," I said, nodding toward the board. "Just like in *The Market Basing Mystery* or *The Second Gong*—make it look like suicide, so no one questions it."

James pinned Janet's name to the top center of the board. "So, the killer wants us to believe she took her own life."

"Which, if we believe Christie," I said, flipping open *Murder in Mesopotamia*, "is exactly what they want us to think. The locked door is part of the trick. The real question is—how did they get in and out without anyone noticing?"

Antonio gave a low whistle. "And we're up against someone who reads mysteries for fun."

I watched them – James arranging the books with librarian-level precision, Thomas dramatically uncapping markers like he was defusing a bomb, Antonio whispering theories that somehow involved poisoned tea, and Agatha pacing the room like she was waiting for someone to drop a real clue.

They were so sure. So earnest. So *excited*.

And maybe… just maybe, I was too.

Janet had died peacefully, according to the coroner. Locked door, no mess, no drama. But The Sleuths weren't buying it—and deep down, I didn't want to dismiss them just yet. Not because I believed it was murder. Not exactly. But because, for the first time in a long while, the idea of playing detective again didn't feel overwhelming—it felt oddly comforting.

Miss Marple always said people notice more when they're not being watched. So I wouldn't announce my suspicions. Not yet. I'd just observe. Collect. And let them think I was fully on board.

Because if this *was* something… I wanted to be ready.

And if it wasn't?

Well, it wouldn't be the first time someone solved a mystery that didn't technically exist.

"Oh," I said, tapping the stack of books. "They don't just read them. They're *using* them."

Randolph raised a hand. "Please tell me this doesn't end with a séance and someone vanishing in a puff of smoke."

"Only if the next murder happens during book club," I muttered.

They all looked at me.

"I was joking," I added. Mostly.

Thomas wrote Brett's name in blue ink on the murder board.

"That's pretty far-fetched," Randolph added.

"You don't think a son could kill his mother?" James asked as he thumbed through *The Murder of Roger Ackroyd*. "Have you read any of my books? Or these?" He pointed with a flourish at the stacks on the table.

"Oh no that's not what I'm saying at all. I just don't think *he* could. Meaning he wouldn't have the knowledge to kill a person in a locked room and make it look like natural causes."

"Gabby, you need to get in that house and see the crime scene."

"There is no crime scene." I plopped down in my chair and ran my fingers through my hair before pushing up my glasses. "Detective Brandon said it was wasn't murder."

"He's guessing and you know it." Randolph scribbled a timeline on the board, including the book club.

"You don't think a book club member murdered her?" I stood quickly and Agatha, who had taken up residence on my lap, sprung off, her paws slipping on the hard floor.

"We must consider all possibilities. You walked her home from book club." He wrote my name on the board.

"Me? I'm a suspect?" I was incredulous. How could he think I killed Janet?

I rubbed my eyes and readjusted my glasses. I felt as if I had created a monster. A giant four-pronged educated-with-enough-mysteries-to-turn-on-the-creator monster. "Add your names then." I stomped over to the main desk. I glanced at the clock. The kids would be here for story hour in five minutes.

"I've got the egg heads, soil and grass seed set up in the back," Mary said.

Good. At least the kids would be in the back away from the talk of murder. Today's craft was planting grass in hollowed-out heads after we put faces on them. Their hair would grow within a week and the kids could give them a haircut.

"Did you pick out a good spring book to go with the craft?"

"I did." She held up the book, *The Tale of Peter Rabbit* by Beatrix Potter, and waited for approval.

"Perfect."

She beamed .

"I'll come help with the craft if you want to read."

"Really, boss? I can read? Sure. I mean I've only been waiting six months for you to ask me."

"Why didn't you just ask?" I laughed. "I could have let you six months ago."

"You would?"

"Of course," I said.

And then the thought hit me—sharp and unwelcome. *Why didn't Janet's son ask her for money?* I muttered it under my breath, but the question lodged itself firmly in my brain, refusing to let go.

"What?"

"Nothing. I'll be back there in a minute. I need to talk to The Sleuths for a minute."

Agatha followed Mary, probably thinking she had treats.

I joined The Sleuths. Randolph had written their names in green.

"Why did you write your names in green?" I asked instead of saying what I originally came back to say.

"Well, we know we didn't do it, my dear," James explained.

"Do we?" I scanned their faces. "My name's on the board—and it's not in green. If I'm a suspect, so are you. *'We're all capable of murder… in the right circumstances.'*"[1]

"I think we've awakened her Miss Marple," James said gleefully.

I grabbed a marker from the tray and rewrote their names in the correct color. "No, you haven't. She never sleeps."

"That's better," I added. "I came back to ask you a question. Why didn't Janet's son just ask for money?"

"That's it?" Antonio asked, his hand on his forehead as if he were thinking harder than his gray cells could bear.

"What would you do if your grandson needed money?" I asked as I erased the green marker names.

"I give it to him," he removed his hand from his forehead and immediately smacked his mouth with it. "I see what you say, Gabby. You are right."

"The other thing I came to say is the kids are coming in for story hour and...we are having it late today because of Janet's..."

The door chimed and in marched Ned, his arms full of scribbled maps, an empty cooler, and what looked suspiciously like a plastic sausage taped to a stick. He wore his usual khaki vest—today with a handmade "PARK RANGER" badge scrawled in green crayon— and had binoculars bouncing from his neck. "I'm on Sasquatch patrol!" he announced to no one in particular. "He's been stealing food again. Last seen near the circulation desk."

His younger brother followed close behind, stopping to spin in a perfect circle before flinging himself dramatically onto a sheepskin area rug. Their sister toddled in last, dragging a stuffed animal with one arm and clutching a juice box like a prized artifact.

Allison appeared in their wake, effortlessly steering them with a smile and a tote bag large enough to hold a small appliance. Her ponytail was half-slipped from its tie, and there was a trail of grass stuck to the knees of her leggings, but she looked content—happy, even. The kind of mom who could juggle a toddler meltdown, park ranger missions, and a snack schedule without losing her mind or her coffee.

I whispered the instructions. "I don't want to hear the word urder or ill. I left the first letters off in case the kids were listening."

Five year old Ned ran over to me. "Miss Gabby, did you know in my new game Sasquatch I can kill someone by running over them with my taxi."

My mouth hung open for three complete seconds. James reached over and manually closed it. "You were saying?"

I stomped back toward the main desk, swinging my arms. Ned jogged alongside me, trying to keep up as he talked more about the game.

"Yeah, and we can chop down trees like anywhere but sometimes a park ranger comes for you…"

Ned's mom Allison took him by the hand. "Mary is starting the story." She smiled an apologetic smile at me. "Kids and games, right?"

I smiled back. I didn't know about kids and games except for what I learned at the library. I loved talking to kids and learning about what childhood was supposed to be like for two reasons. One, I didn't have a normal childhood. I spend it in the system, learning how to stay safe, not playing games where you chopped down trees and pretend park rangers came for you. Real police were a part of my past in a sort of we-rescued-you-but-you-must-be-bad-because-of-your-genetics sort of way. Two, I wanted my own children but I didn't know if I'd ever attract a man who would want to marry me and have kids altogether. Three, okay math wasn't my strong suit, I didn't want to mess up the children I imagined having someday.

"Boss, I need you!" Mary called from the front of the story hour room. I must have zoned out the entire reading of *Peter Rabbit*. It was time to plant the grass.

She waved a plastic spoon at me.

"Oh, coming."

Ned yelled, "Help me, Miss Gabby. I want to tell you more about my game."

I chuckled. "I would love to hear more about Sasquatch."

Attendance for story hour was down today. Only three other kids had come in, and the two mothers had left us for coffee with The Sleuths. I didn't blame them. I wanted a quiet coffee with them. Not that I didn't love story hour and the kids, it was just my brain would not stop. It was running as if it were a rabid dog chasing its tail. Something was off in this town. Two murders in a year. We didn't kill to solve our problems here. Was it my fault for starting the murder mystery books during the book club?

Or was there something else going on?

I scooped a spoonful of potting soil into the egg absentmindedly.

"Miss Gabby," Ned held his belly and laughed. "You missed the egg."

"Oh!" I looked down at my boots, and sure enough they had a liberal sprinkle of earthy-smelling potting soil. Agatha trotted over and did her sleuthing routine. She began to lick my shoes.

"No puppy, you can't eat dirt." Ned picked her up from her middle and she hung there like a rag doll. "I'll hold her till you wipe off your boots."

Ned's mom, Allison, handed me a wipe and I first brushed the potting soil off with my hands before wiping them. "Thank you. I don't know where my head is."

"I do," she said. "Janet. I mean, I can't believe she's gone. She used to help me with my three."

"How so?"

"When I wanted to go to the grocery store alone, she'd watch the kids for an hour or so."

"Oh yes, she brought them here. They like playing with the Legos and the educational games."

I couldn't believe I'd forgotten that. Janet helped lots of Moms with their kiddos. She'd bring them to the library and then the bakery next door. Why would anyone want to kill such a sweet woman?

"Can I ask you a question Allison?"

"Oh…" she paused. "I feel like one of your sleuths." She clapped her hands together and grinned. Her eyes sparkled with…what was that? Joy?

"Why has attendance at story hour been down lately? I mean, even before today's time change."

Allison leaned in until she was five inches from my nose, her elbows braced on the craft table and a smear of potting soil across her sleeve.

"Is that important?" she asked, glancing around like someone might be hiding the answer behind the paper towel roll.

She swiveled and scanned the kids' area, where little hands were busy scooping dirt into hollowed-out eggshells. Googly eyes stared back from Sharpie faces drawn onto each one like a crowd of confused eggheads waiting for a haircut.

"I don't know. Something just seems off in Maplewood."

She wasn't wrong. Even the grass seed project—usually a guaranteed hit—had fewer eager planters today. Fewer Moms. Fewer voices. Fewer questions about whether the eggs could grow hair *and* eyebrows.

"Well, I think Ruthie is running for Councilman Bernard's empty seat. She's been hosting things for families."

"She came to book club Monday night."

"You think she's just trying to garner support by planning events and showing up to book club?"

"You're very perceptive. Why don't you come to book club?" I asked.

"Oh, that's only for smart career people. Not for stay at home moms like me."

It struck me how quick she was to count herself out—like being a stay-at-home mom meant she needed an invitation just to bring her opinions. In Maplewood, people liked their labels tidy. But if this week had taught me anything, it was that the most underestimated voices usually noticed the most.

"You're smart. You just read Ruthie like a book."

She giggled. "You think so?"

"Yes, I do. Why don't you come next week? Monday night at 6:30 and invite your other mom friends."

"Thank you, Gabby. I will."

"Back to Ruthie…" The rest of our conversation was in ten-second snippets as we helped the kiddos draw faces, pat down soil, and water their egg heads.

Ned held up his eggshell triumphantly. "His name is Eggbert!"

We all laughed, and for a moment, everything felt normal.

But as I reached for the watering can, a thought slid in sideways, quiet and persistent –

If Ruthie was trying to garner support for a town council position by stealing library patrons, she wouldn't get my vote.

CHAPTER 5
MISS MARPLE

AFTER THE STORY hour attendees left, I rejoined The Sleuths. All of them except Antonio had their noses in books. They were reading snippets to each other.

James, amateur dramatist of everything, stood beside the murder board holding a well-worn copy of *Murder on the Orient Express*. He cleared his throat like he was preparing to accept an award. "Allow me to set the tone," he said, and began, *"The impossible could not have happened, therefore the impossible must be possible in spite of appearances."*

He looked up with a triumphant little grin. "Classic locked-room logic. I've used a variation of that line in two of my books."

I didn't bother pointing out that Agatha Christie had used it better—twice.

Randolph leaned against the far end of the whiteboard, flipping through *The Mysterious Affair at Styles* with a finger tucked inside to mark his spot. He wore the same grave expression he probably used during his coroner days when delivering unwelcome news. Without ceremony, he read, *"Instinct is a marvelous thing. It can neither be explained nor ignored."*

He gave me a meaningful glance over the top of the book. "That's why you walked Janet home, Gabby. Instinct told you something was wrong."

I swallowed and looked away, suddenly very aware of the quiet hum of the kids' area just behind us. Agatha padded over and sat on my foot, sensing the shift like she always did.

Then Thomas, our former councilman turned reluctant whiteboard scribe, adjusted his glasses and squinted at the quote he'd underlined on the board from *The Clocks*. His voice was low but sure. *"To every problem, there is a most simple solution."*

He capped his marker with a satisfying click and added, "It's always simpler than we think. But that doesn't mean it's easy."

I looked at the three of them—James with his flair, Randolph with his gut, Thomas with his steadiness—and felt the weight of Janet's absence settle into my chest again.

Maybe it was just a bunch of wild guesses dressed up as detective work.

Or maybe—just maybe—we were chasing clues that weren't even there.

Or maybe we were one step away from cracking a real case.

Antonio joined Thomas at the board, staring at the names. Mine was still on there.

"What are you thinking?" I asked him as I plopped down in a seat.

Antonio was squinting at a book like it had just insulted his mother. Then he jabbed a finger at the page and said, "Here! This one fits. Says, '*Very few of us are what we seem.*'"

He looked up, wide-eyed. "That's about Gabby."

"Excuse me?" I blinked at him.

"Well, you read all the books. You know how to stage a locked-room thing. Maybe you *seem* like a nice librarian, but really…"

James let out a dramatic gasp and clutched his chest.

Randolph groaned. "Antonio, she's the one *trying* to solve the murder."

Antonio held up both hands. "I'm just saying. That Marple lady would never rule herself out."

I stared at him. "I bring you books. And snacks."

"And that's how you lure us in," he muttered, clearly unaware of how close he was to losing cookie privileges for life.

"You could have done it."

"What?"

"I mean, you've read all these books…" He paused, turning to the other sleuths. "Isn't there that Poirot saying —'*Imagination is a bad master and a good servant*'? You'd know how to kill her and then lock the door behind you, Gabby!"

'Thanks Antonio for the vote of confidence."

"Oh, I don't think you did it." He chuckled and patted his ample belly. "I think you *could*. That's why I think you could solve it."

"Oh…" I thought about it for a minute. "If it is murder."

"Do you know what your boyfriend did?" Brittany

stormed in and slammed her leather satchel on the table.

"I don't have a boyfriend," I said, instead of asking what Detective Brandon did.

She plowed on, not acknowledging my denial of my one date with Brandon.

"He called the newspaper and told my editor I had to print a retraction of the article that came out this morning."

This got the Sleuths' attention. "The locked-door murder mystery article?" James slammed a book shut.

"What are you sleuths doing?" Brittany said, changing gears. "You're solving this aren't you?"

"I knew you would…" She turned and examined the board. "Gabby is the main suspect."

"She could have done it," Antonio repeated. "She has read all of those books. Those guys are stumbling around trying to find clues."

"I beg your pardon," James said. "I write mysteries for a living and I'm pretty successful at it."

"Yes, but you are no Miss Marple." Antonio tapped my name with a dry erase marker. "She is."

"Randolph, can you call the new coroner and see what the cause of death was?" Brittany asked. "If it wasn't natural causes I don't have to retract my article. And we can solve the case."

She slid off her light rain jacket and draped it over the chair, then pushed up her sleeves. "Antonio, as usual, you are more on the ball than these over-educated buffoons!"

"I beg your pardon!" Thomas shouted, as he

brought another stack of books to the table and flung them down.

"I'm sorry, Sleuths. It's not your fault I've hit a dry spell and rough patch at work."

"What's going on, my dear?" James asked. He took a seat next to her and patted her on the back as she held her head in her hands and sniffled.

"Ever since my article on the paperless town, I've been dry as an AA meeting."

"That's too bad." Randolph added, "And we accept your apology."

"We do live in a rather quiet, peaceful town," Thomas commented, ever the politician.

"You're right and I love it here. But don't you see… if I'm wrong about this, my boss is going to give my younger, fresh-out-of-college intern more pieces to write about climate change."

"And what's wrong with writing about climate change?" Randolph asked.

"Nothing except it will be her instead of me. Plus I want to write about Maplewood. Not the nation. Something the citizens and community can connect with."

"And maybe put you on the map," James added.

Randolph's phone buzzed. He glanced at the screen, muttered, "Excuse me," and stepped out of the fishbowl room to take the call.

I'd been quiet for the whole discussion about me being the prime suspect and why I should solve this so Brittany could write about it. Wait. If I did solve it—if it was a murder—she would win a Pulitzer and leave for Grandview City.

I stood and stomped a foot. "I'm not solving it."

"You don't want to help me?" Brittany said, a tear slipping down her cheek.

"I do, but not this way."

The door opened again.

"I just got off the phone," Randolph said as he stepped back into the room. "Janet did not die of natural causes."

"You're saying she was murdered?" Brittany hopped to her feet. "Yes! I mean, that's horrible, but yay I don't have to retract my article."

Brittany did her signature "Happy Feet" shuffle—heels tapping, shoulders bouncing, arms loose like overcooked spaghetti. It was the dance she saved for good news moments: cleared investigations, fresh leads, or library bake sales with extra lemon bars. Agatha joined her, hopping on her hind legs like a kangaroo.

Then she stopped suddenly, almost tripping over Agatha. "But you'll help me, won't you Gabby? Solve this I mean."

"You can count on us, my dear." James gave me a pleading look. "Of course Gabby will help you save your career and solve the murder."

"Yes, she is your best friend," Antonio added as he patted me on the shoulder. "Right?"

Randolph had returned to the stack of books, flipping through the pages with a furrowed brow. He muttered to himself, then looked up, adjusting his glasses.

"Listen to this," he said, reading aloud. "*Gentlemen, I have always found that it is wise to look on the less obvious side of things.*" [1]

Thomas nodded in agreement. "That's precisely

why Miss Marple offers her insights. Even when others dismiss her, she knows the importance of finding the less obvious facts."

"I'm not Miss Marple and I'm not helping..." It was my turn to storm. I planned to run out to the parking lot at the back of the building and hide in my VW bug for the rest of the day. If Brittany got some sort of award again, she'd leave me and I'd be alone. An orphan once more.

I didn't make it to the back door without Agatha, of course. Brittany's dance had convinced Agatha that it was play time. She nipped at the hem of my plaid pants and ran a circle around me. I caught myself on a cart of used books, slated for the burn pile.

I managed to steady myself, barely—and that's when she doubled back.

As she took another turn around me, I tripped and landed on the hardwood floor. Blood spurted from my nose as it smacked on the floor. I pushed up on one arm like a kickstand.

The back door to the library opened and sets of black boots marched in.

I glanced down instinctively—old habit. The boots were standard issue, scuffed and mud-streaked from walking the perimeter of Maplewood Park.

But Detective Brandon's? His boots were different. Sleek black tactical lace-ups—quiet, no-nonsense, and broken in just enough to show he'd been putting in the miles. Not flashy, but solid. The kind of boots that could step through a crime scene or a church potluck without raising eyebrows.

I sat up and leaned against the bookshelf as I fished

in my cardigan pocket for a tissue. I blotted the blood streaming out of my nose, but not before it soaked my shirt. I glanced down at the blob of crimson soaking up the fabric where my heart was.

"Gabby Keats, you are under arrest for the murder of Janet Kessler." Detective Brandon reached for my elbow.

"It looks as if she needs medical treatment," Officer Greg said.

At the words "medical treatment," a camera shutter clicked. Brittany snapped twenty photos of the detective and me. In the last few, I had a hand in front of my face. A classic sign of guilt. It was as if I was saying "yes I did it. I'm guilty and I'm so ashamed I don't want anyone to see my face."

"I'm okay," I said to the Sleuths, who had now gathered around me at the back of the library.

"I think she may need the nose cauterized," Randolph suggested as he looked up my nose.

"No. I think it stopped." Being driven to the hospital in a police car was not on my bucket list.

"I'm fine everyone. *Really*."

"You'll have to come with me," Brandon said with exactly zero compassion in his voice.

"You don't really think she did it?" Antonio stepped in between me and the detective. "I mean she could have done it."

"Stop talking, Antonio," Brittany ordered.

The Sleuths continued to argue with the detective. I was panicking and shutting down. I was led outside to the parking lot where a fresh rain had fallen. The soil around the back entrance burst with fresh daffodils and let out an earthy spring smell. The door to the library slammed shut, leaving the only friends and family I had on the inside. And me, once again… alone… and being stuffed in the back of a police car like a criminal.

The back door swung open. I turned to see Brittany step out with Agatha in her arms. "I guess I don't have to print a retraction," she said to the detective as he kept one hand on my head and loaded me into the back seat.

"Don't worry, I'll take care of Agatha," she added, and waved one of Agatha's paws at me. "The Sleuths and I will solve Janet's locked-door murder."

"Excuse me," I shoved the detective aside and stood. I shouted over the top of the police car. "No. You won't. I will solve it. Alone. As in without you."

She stumbled back as if I'd shot her. "Gabby… I…"

There was no way I was going to prison so my ex-best friend could write about it, get her article picked up by the Associated Press and move away.

I slipped back into the back seat.

"I'm ready," I said to the detective without looking at his face.

"Gabby, I…" he started.

I'd had enough "Gabby, I…" to last a lifetime. *"Gabby I wish we could keep you. Gabby I wish you were into sports. Gabby I need to tell you that your mother…"*

"Can we just get on with this?" I slammed my back into the seat, and a fresh trickle of blood streamed into my mouth. I pulled out a fresh tissue, held it on my nose, and leaned back.

"The depravity of human nature is unbelievable."[2]

Miss Marple wasn't wrong. But she made it sound

like it crept in slowly, like rot you didn't notice until it hollowed something out.

Mine wasn't slow. My slope had been steep—quick and sharp, the kind you don't walk down, you tumble. And now I was here, helping The Sleuths chase shadows in a library that used to be my safe place.

Maybe after this case—whatever *this* was—I'd be the one to leave. Start fresh. Let Brittany chase her dream, while I figured out if I still had one.

CHAPTER 6
GABBY, THE MISDIRECT

I WASN'T any help to Detective Dexter. I told and retold the story of walking Janet home. She had set her candle down on the porch floor along with her bag as she had pulled out a piece of paper with a new code for the security lock her son had installed. She had punched in the code.

"I don't think I'll ever get used to this Gabby. Putting codes in a lock instead of using a key. Seems like anyone could figure out a code, am I right?"

I had assured her she was safe and the keypads were the way to go. I had one.

"And didn't that crazy Alexa Monroe break into your house and tie up Brittany?" The keypad had beeped and she had reached for her bag.

"I still get a kick out of the fact that you conked her on the head with a Smith Corona typewriter."

"Don't forget your candle," I had reminded her and had handed it to her.

"New fangled isn't always better or safer."

Then she had gone inside and shut the door. I had left. The end.

If only it *had* been the end.

Detective Brandon leaned forward with his elbows on his knees. He had placed me in a comfortable room with arm chairs and a fancy coffee maker. Not an interrogation room.

"You don't really think I did it? Do you?" I took a sip of my coffee with frothed heavy cream on top.

A paramedic had looked at my nose which had stopped bleeding, and cleaned my face with a steaming hot cloth. *Thank you, paramedic, for not letting me parade around the police station looking like a deranged psycho with blood spurting out of my nose.*

"No, I don't think you killed your friend Janet."

"Then why am I here?" I set my coffee down and paced around the room, taking a moment to peer outside the glass wall at the hub. I saw a murder board—with Janet's son's name pinned at the top.

He shifted in his chair uncomfortably and grasped his hands on the table. His knuckles turned white. "I arrested you because I'm following police procedure."

I stared at his white knuckles. "I'll believe that when Agatha stops begging for treats."

"I think we got off on the wrong foot…"

"What do you mean the wrong foot? We've known each other for three months. The time for introductions is over."

He stood and paced back and forth in front of the coffee bar. "I mean with this arrest."

"Is there a right foot when you arrest the girl you

took out on one date and then ignored for two and a half months?"

"I've been busy with all the…" He waved his hand around the practically empty police headquarters.

Desk Sergeant Bob stuck his head in the door. "Oh banana nut muffins. Sally must have dropped by." He whizzed past the detective and grabbed two and a napkin. He took a mug from the mug tree and poured himself a cup of coffee.

"Gabby, is that murder mystery my wife asked for in yet?"

"The M. C. Beaton Agatha Raisin novel - *The Quiche Of Death*?"

"Yeah, I can stop by the library and pick it up for her tomorrow if you have it."

"If I'm not in a cell." I stared at Detective Brandon with my best laser death beams.

Desk Sergeant Bob set his coffee down so hard it slopped over the edges and made a muddy brown puddle on the white counter.

"You think Gabby murdered Janet?" He held his belly like Santa Claus and laughed so hard, I thought the bite of muffin he'd just taken would come back up and lodge in his esophagus.

"No, I don't think she murdered Janet. I want her help."

"Why didn't you just ask her?" Bob rolled a paper towel off the roll and sopped up his coffee mess. "Gabby is the nicest, most helpful person in town."

"You aren't going to tell anyone about this…" Detective Brandon said with a pleading look.

"Did you arrest her at the library?" He set down the

soppy paper towels and checked his watch. "In front of The Sleuths?"

"And Brittany," I added, knowing she would probably be working on an article as we spoke, about the town librarian being arrested for murder or something of the sort.

Bob chucked his paper towel into the trash, then ran his pinched fingers across his mouth in an exaggerated zip.

"Your secret is safe with me." As he exited the room, he turned and said, "But I'm sure the whole town knows if Brittany and The Sleuths were at the library."

After Bob left, I turned to Detective Brandon. "You really just wanted my help?"

"Yes," he said sheepishly.

"Before I agree, and *if* I agree, I want to know why there wasn't any second date…or third."

This wasn't like me at all. I usually just went with the flow and kept my head down. But the events at the library had stirred some new feelings, or maybe awakened old ones in a new way. When it came to survival mode, fight, flight, freeze, or fawn, I usually went with the last two fs. Freeze, not say anything and hope and pray things change without me having to do anything. Or fawn, people please until everyone around me seems satisfied and I feel smaller and insignificant. But now I was ready to try out flight — move away, or fight – like right now with the handsome detective who clearly wasn't interested in me anymore.

"Was it me?" I pointed to my vintage plaid pants that made my legs look like plaid Easter eggs. "Or maybe I'm just not good enough?"

"What…" He took me by my elbows and brushed a wisp of hair out of my eyes. I adjusted my glasses and waited. He dropped my elbows and paced around the room, circling the comfy chairs we'd been sitting in, only minutes before.

"I… well… I'm not as smart as you."

"What?" I dropped my arms to my sides in disbelief.

He stopped short in front of me and gazed into my eyes. "You… intimidate me."

I stumbled backwards and caught myself on the coffee counter. Dizzy from his confession and trying to put it in the right cubicle of my confused brain.

"Didn't you take down the Clockwork Killer?"

"Gabby, it took me five years."

"Yes, but you did it."

"You solved Councilman Bernard's murder in less than twenty-four hours." He sat down heavily. "And you and The Sleuths all have these super brains. Well, except…"

"Antonio," I finished for him. "But he has a different sort of smarts."

"He says you could have murdered Janet." He gave me a quick smile, his dimples … it sent shivers up my spine.

I forgot our argument or whatever we were having for a moment and said, "But you see, he is right. Whoever murdered Janet had to know how to do it. The murderer had to have knowledge of how to commit a locked-room murder."

"Oh, he is right. Not you though."

"Not funny. Next time you want my help, or The

Sleuths' help, just ask. You might want to tell them how intelligent they are."

"Not happening. I have to keep some sort of dignity and authority. Besides, they like me playing the evil detective—like, who's one of them in your mysteries?"

"Inspector Japp," I offered, already knowing where this was going.

"Yes! Inspector Japp." He puffed up slightly. "That's the guy. Scotland Yard. Tough, no-nonsense, always getting things done. He walks into the room and everyone straightens up. Black hair, sharp eyes—ferret-faced, they say, but in a good way. He doesn't waste time on fluff or feelings. He gets to the point, lays down the law. That's me."

I nodded, doing my best not to smile. "Absolutely. You've got the stride and the stare."

He looked pleased with himself, folding his arms. "He's the real backbone of those stories, you know. Keeps things grounded."

I hummed in agreement. No need to tell him Japp usually got the facts wrong until Poirot untangled the truth. He didn't need to know I was more the egg-shaped oddball in the room.

Some truths were better left unspoken. For now.

Before we could finish the conversation Desk Sergeant Bob stuck his head back in the door. He was munching on a muffin. A trail of crumbs fell from his mouth and settled on his rotund belly. My first thought – Agatha would help him clean up those crumbs if she were here.

"The officers brought Janet's son, Brett, in for questioning." As he spoke, the same officers,Greg and

Shane, who had been at the library earlier, led Brett by in handcuffs. Shane gave me a quick wave.

I stepped out of the room and walked to the murder board.

"You think her son murdered her for the money he could get out of her house?" I pointed at his picture. "He's had money troubles."

"So I've learned." Brandon joined me at the board.

"So am I here to help you question him?"

"You know everyone in this town. They haven't warmed up to me yet."

"You might try throwing out a compliment here and there." Then in a rash moment, I punched him in the shoulder. "And not arresting sleuths you want help from."

"Sorry about that."

"I'll help question him if you tell me what killed Janet."

"The coroner says arsenic poisoning."

"Oh," I said.

We walked into the interrogation room, which was a tad nicer than on the cop shows. First of all, the walls had a fresh coat of green paint. And there was lighting. Not a single bulb or blinking fluorescent light.

"Gabby, I didn't know you joined the police," Brett said, his face twisted in a skeptical half-smile.

"I'm consulting on this case."

"I heard you were the main suspect."

"My arrest was a misdirect."

"What?" Beads of sweat formed on his forehead and danced on his bushy eyebrows.

"Brett, don't you have coffee with your mother every morning at her house at six-thirty?"

"I did, yes. I liked to check on her before I went to work." He rubbed the beads of sweat with the sleeve of his jacket—a wrinkled windbreaker, faded at the seams, the kind you throw on when you're already late. His polo shirt underneath was stained near the hem, and his jeans were sagging at the knees, like they'd been worn one day too many. He looked like a man who hadn't planned on being questioned today—shaken, yes, but also tired. Worn down in ways that weren't just about grief. "I can't believe she's gone."

I shook my head toward the door as Brandon moved from behind me.

He joined me outside the room.

"If you give someone small doses of arsenic over time, it can kill them."

"So it could be him."

"I don't know. It could be him just as much as it could be me."

"What do you mean?"

"I mean he loved his mom. He put a new lock on her door with a keypad to make her feel more secure. He stopped by every day to check on her."

"Everything you just said points to him as the murderer. Especially if you include his money troubles."

"Those are motives for sure. But you are looking at this procedurally."

"How else am I supposed to look at it?"

"Relationally. He was devoted to her. They had a loving relationship."

"You can't write 'they had a great relationship' down on paper to excuse someone of murder."

"Of course you can't. But when you consider arsenic in coffee over a long period of time… that's premeditated."

"I can see you have more to say."

"Can I ask him another question or two first, before I tell you?"

"Yes."

We both went back in and sat down.

"When did your money troubles start?" I asked.

"Last month." He stood. "Wait, you don't think I killed my mother for the money, do you?"

"It wouldn't be the first time someone murdered for their inheritance."

Brett plopped back down and chuckled. "There is no inheritance. I was stressed about money, sure, but I needed the money to care for my mother. She asked me to sell her house."

Detective Brandon's phone buzzed. He picked it up and read the text.

"Gabby, Ruthie is dead."

"Do you think the book club has a serial killer?" I asked before I thought about what I was saying in front of Brett.

"My guess would be Owen," I continued. "I wouldn't put it past him to murder a bunch of people so he could write his best selling novel." I covered my mouth, wishing I wouldn't have thrown my theory out so quickly.

Brett stood. "May I go?"

"Not yet," Detective Brandon said. "Not until I figure out whether you are telling the truth or not."

CHAPTER 7

THE CHALLENGE

"RUTHIE IS DEAD?" I asked, my voice cracking on the last word.

"We'll have to continue this conversation later," Brandon said as he grabbed his coat off the hook, his movements sharp and hurried.

I crossed my arms, planting myself like a kid refusing to leave the story hour rug. "I asked you a question. Didn't you ask me here to help you?"

He froze with his coat in mid-air. "Yes, I did." His eyes flicked to mine, guilt flashing before he shoved his arm into a sleeve. "Old habits."

I pushed to stand but froze halfway, caught in an awkward squat that made me feel completely ridiculous. "So that means you want me to come?"

"Yes. Yes." He grabbed my coat off the rack and shoved it toward me, nearly knocking me off balance. "Let's go."

Ruthie hadn't been murdered in a locked room, so

there went The Sleuths' theory of a locked-door killer. I hurried after Brandon and climbed into the SUV behind him, my mind already racing as I reviewed all the info from the first murder. I needed to be careful to separate the two murders in my mind. One may have nothing to do with the other. It's possible someone didn't want Ruthie to get that town council seat.

Brandon turned the blinker on as he pulled onto the street that led to the town square. "What are you thinking?"

Instead of answering his question, I replied, "Are you going to the town square?" My eyes narrowed. "Hmmmm. My theory may be correct then."

"Your theory? We haven't seen the crime scene yet."

In my best Miss Marple voice, I said, "Murders are about motives. Crime scenes are the clues to how-dunnit, not always who-dunnit."

Brandon parked at the town square where a white gazebo stood like a ghostly silhouette, EMTs bent over a body beneath it. He shifted in his seat and gazed at me, his face suddenly somber. "You know who killed her already?"

"Of course not. I'm not a psychic."

"What do you know then?"

"Ruthie was running for a town council seat, the one vacated by Bernard."

"Oh?"

"Yes, and we all know what happened to him." I dragged a finger across my throat, the gesture feeling more ominous than I intended.

"You think someone is killing off town councilmen? Like a serial killer?"

"No, I think someone didn't want Ruthie to have that kind of power. Maybe she had a worse agenda than Bernard did."

"Such as?"

I shrugged. "I have no idea." I opened my door and stepped out, my feet crunching on the gravel. Brandon did the same on his side.

We were about ten steps from the gazebo when the new coroner called, "Detective Brandon, I think we can rule this one a homicide."

I turned and saw Dr. Emory Finch, the town's newest coroner, standing near Ruthie's body. His long, gangly arms hung awkwardly by his sides, making him look like a giant bird. His small wire-rimmed glasses were perched precariously on his long nose, clearly too small for his head, and he pushed them up nervously as he spoke.

"Who called you in so quickly?" Brandon asked, his voice tinged with suspicion.

Dr. Finch's face brightened, his pale cheeks flushing. "Oh, uh, I was already at the morgue. I don't get out much," he admitted, his voice a bit too eager. "When the call came in, I thought… well, I thought I'd get here fast. See it firsthand. Helps with the report." He adjusted his glasses again, his eyes flicking to me and then away, as if unsure where to look.

He looked excited—too excited, honestly. I recognized that look. He was desperate to fit in, to be part of something.

He moved toward Ruthie's body, his long limbs flopping as he walked.

"See the discoloration on her lips? Blue. Likely cyanosis. I'd wager she was poisoned," I said.

He paused and glanced at me, his eyes wide behind those tiny glasses. "I, uh, I read about poisons. Fascinating stuff. Not, um, that murder is fascinating… I mean, it's tragic. Very tragic."

I bit back a smile. He was nervous, socially awkward, but endearing. The way he tried too hard reminded me of a puppy trying to impress its owner.

"She may be right," Emory said, nodding enthusiastically as he pushed his glasses up again. "See the bluish tint? Classic sign. And the body… well, it was definitely moved here postmortem."

My heart skipped a beat. "See. See." I dragged the last 'e' out, flapping my arms like a pigeon. Emory's eyes widened, his mouth forming an 'O' of surprise.

"See what?" he asked, his voice filled with curiosity.

"She has a theory already," Brandon huffed. "She's got a motive for Ruthie's death before even seeing the body."

Emory's eyes sparkled with intrigue. "A theory? Oh, I'd love to hear it. I've been reading Agatha Christie, you know. The Sleuths invited me to their meetings. Fascinating group… They talk about murder daily!"

"The Sleuths are not detectives," Brandon growled, his shoulders tensing.

Emory shrank back slightly but quickly recovered, his excitement returning. "I, uh, they also invited me to the book club. Said you'd be there." He looked at me, his eyes shining with hope.

"Please come," I said, a smile tugging at my lips. "It would be nice to have another coroner in the group."

"Oh, yes. Yes, of course. I'll bring notes! I mean, I'll be there. Socializing. With… people." His long arms flopped nervously at his sides as he beamed at me.

Brandon groaned. "Dead body. Focus, people!"

Emory's face turned beet red. "Right. Yes. Body. Poison. Moved postmortem," he stammered, his voice cracking.

As he fumbled to regain his composure, I couldn't help but like him. A geeky coroner with a big heart who just wanted to belong. Maybe he'd fit right in with The Sleuths after all.

—————

I tightened my coat, feeling the cold bite of the wind. "And… I'll get back to the library. Doesn't look like you need my help." I turned quickly, splashing through a mud puddle. One, because I wasn't watching where I was going, and two, because I needed to get back to the library and check a few Agatha Christie books. Something about these two murders felt familiar, like a mystery I'd read before. It rolled around in my head like marbles but didn't make any sense. Yet.

I could see rearranging the murder board in my immediate future. I would figure out who killed Janet and Ruthie, how they were connected, and who had motive to murder both of them.

I left the gazebo, crossed the square and the street, then made my way down the alley to the back door. I opened it and hung up my coat, my fingers stiff from the cold.

"Oh my dear, you're back. We were so worried." I

stepped out of the murder mystery section and froze. The Sleuths and Brittany all stood with worried and expectant looks. Oh. I'd forgotten I'd been arrested.

"You didn't answer my texts," Brittany chided, waving her phone around above her head, her blonde curls bouncing with each movement.

"We were so worried," Antonio stepped forward, wrapping his doughy, basil-scented arms around me and squeezing. My stomach growled, a not-so-subtle reminder that I hadn't eaten.

I fished around in my messenger bag for my phone. "Oh, it was confiscated at the police station."

"Oh," Antonio said, releasing me from his hug and stepping back. "So you escaped. On the run. We'll help you…" he paused, his eyes scanning my face for clues. "My cousin Vinny, he…"

"No, Antonio. Thank you. Although I appreciate your offer to hide me off the grid, I'm free. They let me go."

Brittany snapped ten photos of me. "Police brutality. That's what the headline will read."

"No. No." That's when I noticed the murder board. It took up the entire wall, strings of yarn connecting photos of Janet, newspaper clippings, and hand-written notes. "You were going to solve this without me?"

James patted me on the shoulder. "My dear, you read this all wrong. We were going to solve this for you. If you remember correctly, you were arrested for murdering Janet."

"Not really."

"What do you mean?" Thomas asked, his eyes

narrowing as he leaned against the bookshelf, arms crossed.

"Detective Brandon wanted my help, but he was too proud to ask." I couldn't help the red tint that crept onto my face.

"Do tell," James leaned in, intrigue written all over his face, his fingers twitched as if ready to take notes.

I dropped my bag on the table and sank into my favorite chair, feeling the weight of the day settle into my bones. Agatha leaped onto my lap, her tail wagging furiously as she burrowed her head under my arm, demanding affection. I scratched behind her ears, feeling her soft fur beneath my fingers. Her warmth grounded me, pulling me back to the present.

"Not until I get a cup of your magic espresso." I leaned back, letting Agatha curl up, her tiny body fitting perfectly on my lap.

"Coming right up," James said, already bustling over to the table where the coffee machine sat, his movements swift and practiced.

While he made my coffee, I studied the board. The Sleuths had been busy. They'd outlined possible motives, suspects, and timelines for Janet's murder.

My mind raced. Why would someone kill Janet and Ruthie? Political power. That was the connection. But who would kill over a town council seat?

Brittany scrolled on her phone, her brow furrowed. Suddenly, she jumped up, her chair scraping against the floor. "Way to bury the headline, Gabby!"

I looked up, startled. "What are you talking about?"

"There's been another murder." Her eyes were wide, her face pale.

My heart skipped a beat. "Who?"

"Not who. Where." She turned her phone toward me, the screen showing a live news feed of the town square. Police tape surrounded the white gazebo, Detective Brandon standing with his arms crossed, his face a storm cloud of anger and determination.

Whoops. I'd been so busy trying to figure out why someone would kill Ruthie, I forgot to mention she'd been murdered. "That's Ruthie's crime scene."

There was a beat of silence.

Four heads snapped toward me.

"You *knew*?" they all gasped in unison—more surprise than accusation, but still enough to make me sink a little lower in my chair.

Antonio puffed out a huge sigh. "That means you didn't do it. Being in jail is a good alibi."

I barely heard him. My eyes were glued to the screen, my mind connecting threads faster than I could process them. I knew that scene. I'd read it before.

The marbles in my head stopped rolling and clicked into place. It was a reenactment. The killer was playing out a scene from an Agatha Christie novel. But which one?

I jumped up, nearly knocking Agatha off my lap. She yipped in protest, her tiny paws slipping as she tried to regain her balance. "I need every Agatha Christie book we have. Now!"

The Sleuths sprang into action, moving faster than I'd ever seen them. Books flew off shelves, landing on the table in front of me. I scanned titles, my fingers flipping through pages as if they held the answers to everything.

My heart raced as I pieced together the puzzle. Two murders. Both staged like scenes from classic mysteries. The killer wasn't just killing. They were sending a message.

I swallowed hard, a chill crawling up my spine. This wasn't just about power. This was about playing the perfect game. And they'd invited me to play.

I looked up at the murder board, my eyes narrowing as I took in the tangled web of yarn and paper. "It's not just about who did it. It's about why. They're reenacting scenes. They're following a script."

Brittany's eyes widened. "A script? You mean… like a book?"

I nodded, my heart pounding. "Exactly. And if I don't figure out which one, there's going to be another murder."

James handed me a cup of espresso, his hands trembling slightly. "Who would do something like that?"

"That's what I'm going to find out." I took a long sip of the espresso, letting the warmth steady my nerves. "We're dealing with someone who thinks they're the perfect storyteller. And they're copying Christie books to write their own murder mystery. One chapter at a time."

I met the eyes of each member of The Sleuths, their faces a mix of fear and determination. "And if we don't solve it first, they're going to write the final chapter."

The room fell silent, the weight of the truth settling over us like a shroud.

I looked at the murder board one more time, my jaw clenching with resolve. This wasn't just a mystery. This was a battle of wits. And the killer had just made their move.

It was my turn to make mine.

I picked up the first Agatha Christie book from the pile - *The Body in the Library* - and opened it to the first page.

CHAPTER 8
THE AGATHA CHRISTIE COPYCAT KILLER

"LET ME GET THIS STRAIGHT, you think there is a serial killer, copying murders from murder mystery novels?" Brittany asked.

I looked up from *The Body in the Library* I'd been flipping through. "Not just any murder mystery novels. Agatha Christie's Miss Marple novels."

Thomas cleared his throat. "As a former councilman, I'd like to help solve Ruthie's murder. Not because I liked her. Just because it's the right thing to do..." His voice trailed off.

James took over. "What you are saying is that you fear there is a different sort of serial killer on the loose. One who is murdering anyone connected with the town council, past, present, or future."

"And you are next," Antonio interjected with a little too much enthusiasm.

"How did you know, James?" Thomas asked, his face drained of color.

"I've written a few murder mysteries myself." That

was an understatement. James was the first to remind everyone he'd written over fifty mystery novels. His humble-beginnings claim to fame was that he had written his first best-seller here at the library on a manual Smith Corona typewriter.

Randolph added, "I've invited Dr. Emory to join the Sleuths and the book club. Maybe we can get some more information from him tomorrow."

"I'm glad. Not only will he be a great asset, but I think he needs some friends." I dropped my gaze and continued to leaf through *The Body in the Library*.

Agatha leaped up from where she'd been curled at my feet and ran three excited circles around the table, tail wagging like she'd cracked the case wide open. Brittany interrupted my research by chasing her and then skidding to a stop in front of Thomas. She pulled out her phone.

Brittany moved closer to Thomas and pushed the record button on her phone app. "Can I get a statement from you, Thomas? About your theory, I mean."

He stumbled backward as if she had jabbed him with a knife. "Absolutely not. I'm not putting out a half-baked theory and putting a target on my back."

"I thought you already had a target on your back," Antonio chuckled. "This story will get you the job in Grandview City, right Brittany?"

"My dear girl, let's not get ahead of ourselves. The worst thing a journalist can do is print something she has to retract later."

I could tell by the reddish tinge on Brittany's cheeks that the comment stung. She shoved her phone back in her pocket and dropped into a chair. Agatha took the opportunity to lick her shoes.

James closed the short distance between him and Gabby in three long strides. "Oh my dear, we want to help you …" He paused and looked around the group.

We each nodded in approval. Except me. I half-nodded which probably came off more as a wobble like on a bobble head. I couldn't say yes, I couldn't lose her. She was my family. I was at a crossroads. I could use the knowledge I had of the Miss Marple mysteries and solve the case, getting Janet and Ruthie the justice they deserved and stop a killer. But if I was successful, that meant Brittany would write the piece, getting her the accolades and job she deserved.

If I solved it, everyone won. Possibly Thomas, if his "half-baked" theory was right. Justice won. Brittany won. The Sleuths won. Everyone won. Except me. Once again. My loss was everyone else's gain. Because if I was right, the case would be closed, the town would move on, and I'd be left exactly where I always ended up—on the outside, watching people walk away like they always did. My mom. The social workers. The foster families. Everyone leaves.

While everyone else chatted, I made the choice. Actually, I found the passage I'd been looking for.

I stood and waved the book in the air. "Listen guys, I think this is key to Ruthie's murder."

"What is?" Britany sprang out of her chair, her interest and energy renewed.

"Oh! The body in the library wasn't even who they thought—it was this poor Girl Guide named Pamela, dressed up to look like a dancer named Ruby, and her body was moved—just like I think Ruthie's was. Twisted, right?"

"And...? Don't leave us hanging my dear," James said.

"In *The Body In The Library*, the body is moved to throw the police off the scent of the real killer." I ran to the board and scribbled the name of the book and wrote Ruthie's name under it.

I turned back to The Sleuths and said, "It's seven in the morning and the Bantrys find a dead girl in their library—just lying there in an evening dress with smeared makeup like she wandered out of a party and into a crime scene. No one knows who she is or how she got there. Then another body turns up—burned beyond recognition in a quarry. Two girls, two deaths... and Miss Marple's the only one asking the right questions."

"I see," Brittany said. "Someone is using a misdirect or red herring or whatever you call it."

Antonio clapped his hands together and exclaimed, "They are throwing the fish so we look at the fish instead of the killer."

"I couldn't have said it better myself, my good man." James clapped Antonio on the back so hard, he went tumbling forward.

"Do you have a Miss Marple novel for Janet's murder?" Randolph asked, always the logical non-emotional Sleuth. I guess you had to have more logic than emotions to be a coroner.

"Yes, I think I do." I shoved the *The Body In The Library* into Brittany's hand and commanded, "Mark my place. I'll be right back."

I ran back to the mystery section, weaving between the tables piled high with the Miss Marple books The Sleuths had already pulled. My eyes scanned the shelves, searching for any they'd missed—the ones I knew were important.

I closed my eyes for a second, letting muscle memory take over. I knew where every Agatha Christie novel sat by heart. It was a challenge I'd given myself back in high school—finding them blindfolded—after spending hours here, or at Brittany's house after school.

I opened my eyes and reached for the last spot where it should've been.

"Uh, guys? We have a problem." I turned toward them, heart sinking. "The book I'm looking for is gone. The one we're reading for book club—*A Murder Is Announced*."

The Sleuths joined me in the narrow aisle with James leading the way.

"Don't you have more than one copy?" James asked. "You have several copies of each of my novels."

Thomas chuckled. "That's because you donate them to the library."

"Exactly," I said as I furiously moved books, checking behind books and moving as far as the M.C. Beaton section.

Brittany joined me and pulled books off the shelf. "Explain exactly as if we know nothing."

"Well, this puts a whole new twist on the crimes," I mumbled to myself as I stacked murder mystery books on the floor.

"I know that in books it is always the most unlikely person. But I never find that rule applies in real life." [1]

"Is this another red herring fish?" Antonio asked from behind Thomas and James, who blocked the aisle.

"She's thinking," James explained, "like a murderer."

I handed a stack of books to James so Agatha wouldn't chew on the ones I'd pulled off the shelf. Although Agatha had grown up in the library, she still preferred chewing on books to reading them. I stood quickly and the blood rushed to wherever it rushes to which makes you faint. I steadied myself on the bookshelf.

I had a sudden sickening thought. "Antonio, go check Agatha's bed for *A Murder Is Announced.*"

He complied, yelling over his shoulder as he waddled out of the murder mystery aisle. "You think the puppy took the red herring book?"

"Yes, I do. We all know she likes to chew books"

"She no take it. No book here." Antonio yelled from the corner of the library that housed Agatha's maroon pillow.

Agatha relocated in front of James, hoping a book would fall off his stack that was now precariously leaning. The slightest move would cause the whole stack to fall on her head.

Agatha leaped like the books were made of bacon—tail wagging, feet skittering, absolutely persuaded it belonged to her. James jerked the stack closer to his chest with a strangled yelp. "It's *not* food, Agatha!" he hissed.

Then he added, "Agatha my dear, you are not helping your cause here. I'll give you a leather journal to chew on." James tottered backward as Agatha leaped again, and Randolph rescued him by taking half the stack.

"Thank you."

Brittany's hands hung limply at her sides. "I can't find it. I went all the way to the Anne Perry section."

"Are you going to tell us what this is all about?" Thomas asked. "We'd like to get to the business of solving this case."

Antonio joined us again from the opposite side. "Before you are next?"

Antonio wasn't trying to start an argument, but with Thomas fearing for his life, he'd just said exactly the wrong thing.

Thomas lunged forward. I was the cream part of this argument Oreo. With Antonio on one side of me and Thomas on the other in this confined space, a physical fight would mean me getting injured. I still had blood on my shirt from my previous fight with the hardwood floor. I didn't want another injury. Plus fighting wouldn't solve the crime or keep Thomas safe.

Brittany had moved behind Antonio's bulky frame after his statement. She pulled on his shirt and ordered, "Let's move, Antonio."

James tried to sooth Thomas. "I'm sure Antonio didn't mean what he said."

"I just repeat his theory," Antonio defended himself as he backpedaled.

"Okay, guys, let's reshelve these books."

"Everyone out of the aisle, now," Brittany ordered.

I shelved a book. "Meet me at the murder board and I'll explain everything."

Thomas and Randolph exited one side as Brittany continued to drag Antonio out the other.

My voice came out calm, but with that edge I'd perfected after years of dealing with rowdy book club debates. "Honestly, you two—some gentlemen lose all sense the moment someone agrees with them."

James and I finished shelving the books in silence, the kind of comfortable quiet that happens when you've worked with someone long enough to not need to fill the air. The only sounds were the soft hiss of the heating vents and the satisfying slide of spines against wood. Outside the tall arched windows, afternoon sun filtered through a veil of silvery clouds heavy with the threat of rain, cast long shadows across the worn floorboards.

I slid a copy of *The Moving Finger* halfway onto the shelf, hesitated, then asked, "You aren't really going to buy Agatha a journal to chew on, are you?"

James shoved a worn copy of *Five Little Pigs* into place with a bit more force than necessary. The shelf gave a subtle creak of protest.

"Of course not," he said, not looking at me. "Owen left one here the other night. One of his journals—full of scribbles and ramblings. I was going to give her that."

I froze with a slim hardcover suspended in midair, one hand still on the spine. "Did you read it?"

He let out a quiet scoff, adjusting a crooked row of titles like they were personally responsible for his mood. "I don't need to read it. He's shared enough of his 'genius' ideas with me already. Claims he's got this idea that's going to land him an instant bestseller."

I slid the book into place more carefully than necessary, then turned to watch him. "You don't like him, do you?"

"It's not that I don't like him," he said, finally meeting my gaze. "I don't like the idea that he thinks he doesn't have to earn it like the rest of us. No rewrites, no rejections—just success on the first try. Like publishing is some kind of vending machine."

"And yet, he's just spinning his wheels, isn't he?" I asked. "Don't you feel sorry for him?"

James leaned against a bookshelf, arms crossed, eyes flicking briefly to the circulation desk before settling back on me. "I've tried to help him. I really have. But the other night at book club? He got on my last nerve."

"So you're going to let Agatha chew on his journal."

He smirked, the tension around his mouth softening. "Just a few teeth marks. Maybe *The Chewed Journal* could be the title of his bestseller."

I laughed, the sound rising into the rafters like a warm puff of air. "Could I see it?"

"The journal?" he asked, cocking a brow.

Then his expression shifted—subtle, but enough that I straightened.

"After you tell us what's going on with the missing book," he said, voice low and even. "Are you sure somebody didn't just check it out?"

"I'm sure." I shoved the last murder mystery novel on the shelf and turned to him. "Deal."

The rest of The Sleuths had grabbed fresh coffees and were now huddled in front of the murder board. The after-school crowd would be here soon and I didn't want the murder board out in plain sight, or to be discussing murder in front of first graders. So I had to explain quickly.

"Janet donated a first copy edition of *A Murder is Announced* to the library. Bea wanted to keep it in a display case, but Janet insisted it be kept on the shelf for everyone to read."

"What's something like that worth?" Thomas asked. He was probably relieved at the new evidence that maybe the murders were about something other than bumping off town council people.

"Wait," Antonio shouted. "This is the book we are reading for book club."

"Yes, and you had it Monday night," Randolph said evenly, stating an important fact and clue at the same time.

"And now it is missing." Brittany typed notes on her phone.

"Yes, and now we need to move the murder board," I instructed as the activity bus pulled up in front of the library. "The after-school kiddos are here."

Randolph and Antonio wheeled the board to the back hall where we stored it, with the writing toward the wall.

It was then that I realized none of us had eaten lunch and it was three o'clock. The Sleuths had stayed here all day waiting for me to be released from questioning.

———

I watched the activity bus pull up, releasing a swarm of eager faces and high-pitched laughter. My chest tightened. It was only a matter of seconds before they'd be barreling through the doors, expecting story hour and snacks, completely oblivious to the murder board we had just wheeled down the hall. A line of cars carrying parents, pulled down the alleyway to the back parking lot.

I forced myself to smile as I glanced at James. "I'll take a peek at the journal later."

He hesitated, his fingers tightening around the worn leather cover. "I think you should look at it now."

I frowned. "Why?"

He held it out, his voice dropping to a whisper. "Owen scribbled notes about the missing book. You're going to want to see this."

Curiosity got the better of me, and I took the journal from his outstretched hands. As soon as my fingers touched the old leather, a chill ran through me. Owen's handwriting was frantic, nearly illegible, his thoughts scattered across the margins like he was racing against time.

My heart pounded as I scanned the pages. The missing *A Murder is Announced*... theories... suspects... and then a name that made my stomach drop.

The door swung open behind me, and a cold burst of air cut through the library. I looked up, my chest tightening as parents flooded in, faces tense, eyes darting around the room. They moved with purpose, jaws clenched, voices low and sharp as they corralled their kids.

I watched in stunned silence as mothers and fathers grabbed little hands, tugging them toward the exit, no questions, no arguments. The children looked back over their shoulders, eyes wide with confusion. My heart sank as I realized they wouldn't be coming to our after-school story hour for the elementary kids today—or maybe ever again.

I caught snippets of hurried whispers as they filed out the door.

"…arrested for murder…"

"…can't believe she was here with our kids…"

"…not safe…"

My vision blurred, the weight of their words pressing down on my chest. This wasn't just about a missing book or a journal full of scribbled notes. This was about me. About my life crumbling before my eyes.

Gabby the librarian.

Gabby the murderer.

Gabby the monster who fooled everyone.

I could feel my reputation unraveling, thread by fragile thread. Brittany was leaving, and my beloved group of kids—the ones who listened wide-eyed to every story, who ran up to hug me after every session—were being yanked away, their parents shielding them from me like I was something toxic.

I gripped the journal, my knuckles white. I couldn't let it end like this. I wouldn't.

A flash of color outside the window caught my eye. I turned just in time to see Bea, the retired librarian, shuffling up the sidewalk… holding something familiar.

My heart skipped. It was the dust jacket for *A Murder is Announced.*

"What on earth…" I whispered, my pulse quickening. How did she get that? And why now?

Bea looked up, her eyes locking with mine through

the glass. Her expression was unreadable, but the way she clutched that dust jacket... The air shifted—subtle, but sharp. Like the exact moment in a mystery novel when the wrong suspect smiles... and you just know you've been reading the clues all wrong.

I turned to James, my voice trembling. "We need to talk to her. Now."

Before he could answer, the door swung open again, the cold wind sweeping through the empty library. Bea stepped inside, the dust jacket clutched to her chest like a lifeline.

My breath caught, my heart pounding as she slowly approached. I didn't know what she was about to say, but I had a sinking feeling it was going to change everything.

CHAPTER 9
THE EVIDENCE

"GABBY, I'M DISAPPOINTED IN YOU," Bea said as she parted the children exiting the library with their parents.

I was too upset about the children leaving to answer. She took that as a sign that I wanted her to continue.

"Really, I trained you better than this." She waved the book jacket in the air.

"Trained me better than what?" I gulped, trying to stifle the sobs rising up in my belly. As much as I wanted to solve this case and find out who killed Janet and Ruthie, and find the missing book of course, right now I just wanted a good cry followed by chewing out Detective Brandon. He hadn't given a thought to how arresting me was going to affect me, my job, and my standing in the community. If he would have just asked for my help instead of arresting me and hauling me into the police station, none of this would be happening.

"I've got to go work on a story," Brittany explained

apologetically as she swung her satchel over her shoulder and jingled her keys. "Sorry, Gabby."

I nodded my head at her and said nothing. The story would be about me, no doubt. My arrest. Me as a potential suspect. "Crazy murder-obsessed librarian finally goes off her rocker and becomes an Agatha Christie copycat killer."

"What are you talking about?" Bea asked as Brittany slinked out of the library.

"Oh, did I say that out loud?"

"Yes, and not for one second do I think you murdered anyone." Bea shoved the book jacket into James's hand, and at a surprisingly quick pace for an eighty-five year old, sprinted out the door and onto the sidewalk. She grabbed Brittany by the elbow and gave her the famous librarian look while she shook one finger at her. We Sleuths watched as if we were watching a terrible trailer for a movie we would never watch.

Bea stomped back in two minutes later. "This is highly unethical." She said without explanation.

To which James responded, "I don't think we should touch the dust jacket." He held it by one corner with pincher fingers, like a crab.

"Why-ever not?" Bea asked.

"Fingerprints," Randolph said as we all watched the dust jacket in horror, as if it had murdered Janet and Ruthie.

"Not to worry. It needed a good cleaning. It had a cranberry-colored smudge on it, so I wiped it down."

"You what?" I said, eyeing the edges of the book jacket.

"Yes, I found it Tuesday morning on the ground outside the library. I thought you had dropped it."

"Me?" I asked

"During book club you dropped the copy of *A Murder Is Announced* that Janet donated to the library. I told you it should have been in a display case."

That's when Bea noticed James's typed notes on the table—bold title at the top: "Suspects." She swallowed hard and her lips disappeared. "These are all the book club members."

"Yes, my dear. And what you didn't know is that someone stole the copy of *A Murder Is Announced* Monday night," James explained.

Bea sucked her lips in as she slumped into a chair that Antonio provided just in time, before she hit the floor. She pulled a handkerchief out of her tweed trousers and dabbed her nose. "And I wiped away the clue."

I took the moment of silence after her declaration to lock the front door and turn on the closed sign. The last thing I needed was another parent or patron walking in with that look—the one that said they believed Brandon got it right when he arrested me.

Once I rejoined The Sleuths and Bea, I suggested, "Why don't you gentlemen go grab some food and we'll call it a day."

Agatha yipped and ran in three quick circles. "Don't you dare pee here," I chided. "I'll take you out in a minute."

Bea had regained her composure and sat up straight. "I'll go with you, Gabby—and you can tell me what in the *Sam Hill* is going on in Maplewood.

The whole town's acting squirrelly as a soup sandwich."

The Sleuths agreed but only because they saw how distressed I was. Not because they wanted to stop investigating. They left after murmuring some things such as…"praying for you, dear" and "it will be okay, you didn't murder anyone even though the town thinks you did."

"I'll contact Emory and see what he found out," Randolph added.

"I'm going to contact the town council and see if I can get some more information on Ruthie." Which, for Thomas, was code for going to make a few phone calls and then hide out at home just in case there was a serial killer murdering past, present, and future town council people.

———

The sun was shining on the puddles on the sidewalk making them look like mirages in the desert. Agatha made sure she tested every mirage, which meant she splashed water all over my boots and soaked her fur.

"What if this is all a mirage?" I asked Bea.

"You mean a misdirect?" Bea asked. She had been the head librarian and read her share of murder mysteries. Not to mention, she attended the book club, which meant her love of mysteries hadn't fizzled.

"Yes, but I just can't figure out why Detective Brandon thought I murdered Janet."

She linked arms with me. "That young man doesn't think you killed anyone. Any more than Agatha here."

"He said he arrested me to get my help," I said, the words tasting as bitter now as they had then. "But that doesn't undo what it looked like to everyone else. You saw those parents dragging their kids out of the library."

I paused, heat rising in my chest. "He doesn't understand how things work here. How fast word spreads. How hard it is to come back from something like that."

I glanced down at my shoes. "And the way people were looking at me today… I don't know. For a second, I even wondered if maybe they saw something I don't."

"I think after tomorrow's edition of the Maplewood Gazette they will be back."

I stopped in the middle of a puddle. Agatha took the opportunity to roll on her back and bathe in the muddy water.

"What did you say to Brittany?" Was I going to lose Brittany as a friend before she got the job in Grandview City and moved away?

"You know what librarians are good at?" Bea's eyes sparkled, mischief dancing behind her glasses. "Finding facts. And making sure the right story gets told."

I shook my head, splashing through another puddle. "Well, the story they're telling right now is that I'm a murderer. You saw those parents practically dragging their kids out by the ears." My voice cracked, and I swallowed hard, forcing the knot back down my throat.

Bea's smile didn't falter. "You also saw Brittany standing outside the library fifteen minutes ago, arguing with me like her life depended on it. She didn't want to do it, you know."

I froze. "Do what?"

"I told her she owes it to this community to tell the whole story. Not just the gossip, not just the headlines. I told her she needed to write an article about how the local librarian and her loyal Sleuthing Society are going to solve this case and prove the truth."

My heart skipped. "You… you told her to write that?"

"I did. And I pointed a finger at her because she was being stubborn." Bea grinned. "The whole town saw, too. Good. Let them wonder." She patted my arm. "Besides, what better way to get people to read the paper tomorrow?"

I stared at her, a laugh bubbling up before I could stop it. "You're a lot sneakier than you look, Bea."

She winked. "That's how I survived all those years as head librarian." Her voice softened, her hand still warm on my arm. "Gabby, facts are stubborn things. They don't change just because someone decides to believe a lie. And tomorrow, when Brittany's article runs, they'll see the truth. They'll see that you're not giving up. That you're still fighting."

A spark of hope flickered, fragile but growing. "You really think that will change their minds?"

Bea looked down at Agatha, now happily rolling in another puddle. "I think they'll see the truth. And the truth has a way of washing away even the worst mud."

I took a deep breath, the air cold and sharp. Maybe the sun wasn't the only thing breaking through the clouds today.

Maybe, just maybe, the facts would clear my name.

CHAPTER 10
A COFFEE BRIBE AND A SIDE OF BETRAYAL

BEA and I walked around the block a few times, her encouraging me, and me getting just a little bit of hope resurging. If anything was going to happen to clear my name and get the patrons back in the library, I couldn't depend on someone else to do it for me. Sure Brittany had my best interests at heart, but in a way, wasn't everyone out for themselves? I'd learned that through my many years in the foster care system.

I kept the front lights of the library out so if any of The Sleuths passed, they wouldn't knock on the door. Or anyone for that matter. Not that anyone would be knocking after the comments the parents made. I'd already sent the staff home. I set up the murder board in the back of the library before going into the fishbowl room to brew some coffee and a shot of espresso. I hadn't eaten lunch either, and evening was quickly approaching. There was no way I was going to The Tasty Burger for dinner. Looks like I'd be eating muffins for lunch and dinner.

I added Janet's son, Brett, to the murder board alongside all the book club members. Owen didn't have any reason to kill Ruthie. Neither did Brett. But if he took the book thinking it was worth a lot of money, he had motive to kill his mother despite what he said in the police station. What was it Miss Marple said? *"I know that in books it is always the most unlikely person. But I never find that rule applies in real life."*[1]

A few unshelved Agatha Christie books still littered the tables. I picked one up and flipped through it, wondering if there was something inside the missing mystery, *A Murder Is Announced*. Was there a hidden compartment? A message in the pages? Maybe the book wasn't stolen for its plot at all. Maybe it held something else—something only the right eyes would notice. A pinprick here, a mark there... Miss Marple would say people hide the most interesting things in the most ordinary places. I munched on a muffin and sipped coffee as I flipped through more books, holding them up to the light. *You're chasing dead ends, Gabby.* Agatha yipped in agreement as I dropped a chunk of banana nut muffin for her.

Was that blood on the cover? A loud knock interrupted my musings.

I hopped up and set down my coffee carefully. I didn't want to damage any of the books. Agatha beat me to the door. She wagged her whole body in excitement. It must be someone she knew.

Brandon. I glared at him as if he were a mosquito I couldn't quite squash. When I feel the most down and out, he comes buzzing around.

I unlocked and opened the door five inches. "Are you here to arrest me again?"

"What? No… I…"

Agatha squeezed out the door and licked his boots. I opened the door further to let her back in. Brandon mistook the opened door as an invitation to come in.

He entered holding two coffees. "I come in peace."

I crossed my arms. "Peace? You arrested me. You ruined my career"

He glanced around the empty library. "Why are you closed?"

I turned and walked back to my table of books, leaving him holding the coffee. "For a detective, sometimes you don't see what's right in front of you."

He followed me. "I don't follow." He set the coffee down and pulled out a chair.

I swiped at a tear. Did he really not notice the sign on the door? The darkened windows? The way my shoulders hunched like I was carrying the weight of a dozen whispered accusations?

"The after-school story hour parents said awful things."

Their words still clung to me like burrs I couldn't shake.

"Things like 'arrested for murder,' 'can't believe she was here with our kids,' 'not safe,' 'what kind of example does this set for our kids?' They even said I should have stepped down the second I was arrested"

"Wow, I had no idea…"

I let out a bitter laugh. "Brandon, this is a small town. Reputations are everyone's business, and they can rise and fall in an instant. Didn't you stop and think? You arrested the town's head librarian for murder."

I grabbed my coffee and gulped it down, scalding my throat in the process. *Good. Let it burn.* But the sting was nothing compared to the heat of humiliation curling in my gut.

He sighed and ran his hands across the stubble on his cheeks. I pulled a tissue out of my cardigan pocket and blew my nose. It was then that I noticed the dark circles under his eyes.

"I had no idea..." he said again, standing to pace. Agatha joined him.

"Listen, I moved to a small town to have a simpler life. One not so full of..."

"*A Murder is Announced*," I interjected.

He froze. "Was it announced? Are there going to be more?"

"No. It's an Agatha Christie novel—the one the book club has been reading."

"I'm trying to apologize here."

Apologies must not come easy for him.

"I didn't think you were guilty. I needed you on the inside."

I blinked. That's his excuse?!

He hesitated. "I should've asked you for help first. But you wouldn't have stayed out of it anyway."

I stared at him. He's right, but I won't admit it.

I picked up another murder mystery book. "Back to the missing book."

Beads of sweat formed on his forehead. "Am I forgiven or not? Gabby, you know you're important to me. I would never hurt you on purpose..." His words trailed off, and he looked down at his boots, which Agatha had licked clean.

He was trying so hard. *The truth is, we needed each other. No, Gabby, don't hug him. You need him, but not that way. You need his help with the case.*

Too late. I'd wrapped my arms around his waist and squeezed.

For an eternity, I didn't think he was going to hug me back. And then he did. His arms circled me, pulling me in, and I squeaked as he squeezed the air out of me. Then—so softly I barely felt it—he kissed the top of my head.

"Thank God, I thought I blew it."

I would have answered, but I couldn't move. *Scratch that. I didn't want to move.* He loosened his grip just enough for me to breathe, but I wanted to stay here forever. Feeling safe. Feeling— loved?

Where did that come from?

I stepped back, stumbling into a chair. He reached for my hand, steadying me, then pulled me toward him again. His lips brushed mine—so lightly it felt like a butterfly had landed for just a moment.

He stepped back. "Forgiven?"

I had no words. A surge of heat crept from my heart to my face. I croaked, "Yes," and cleared my throat. "Back to the missing book?"

He smoothly switched gears to detective mode, while my gears continued to slip back to the hug. *And the kiss. Get a grip, Gabby.*

The best way to switch gears was to flee. So I did. I ran to my office without an explanation. He didn't follow.

I grabbed the gallon baggie with the *A Murder Is Announced* book cover, took ten deep breaths, and smacked my cheeks with my free hand. *Get a grip. Focus on the case.*

Once I felt a little less butterfly-fluttery, I rejoined him at the table. Only he wasn't there. He was studying the murder board.

"Why are all these people suspects?"

I handed him the baggie. "This is evidence. The book was stolen after, or during, book club the other night."

"And the answer to my question?" He leaned in and studied Janet's son's picture. "I thought we cleared him."

"Of murder? Or theft?"

"I don't follow."

I smiled and chuckled. "I'll explain everything if you give me a chance."

"So, stop interrupting? Got it." He placed the evidence bag on the table with the books and rejoined me at the murder board. "Alrighty, Miss Marple, explain."

"Before I start, Bea—the former head librarian," I said, making sure he had context for who she was, "found the dust jacket outside the library in the alley."

He nodded. "And?"

"She said it had a cranberry-colored smudge on it."

"Blood?"

"You're interrupting."

He held up his hands in surrender.

"She also said she cleaned it with a disinfecting wipe."

"Our…"

I put a finger to my lips to silence him. My stomach took over and filled the gap of silence with a lion-like growl. "Sorry, I haven't eaten all day, except for a few muffins."

I pointed to the table where the crumbs and muffin paper should have been. I turned to Agatha, who immediately hid her face under her paws.

"You ate my crumbs and the wax muffin paper?" I chided. "I'll deal with you later."

Brandon chuckled. "How about I go grab us some dinner and drop this off at the lab on the way?"

"Meet back here?" I wanted to be clear, to make sure I wasn't getting my wires crossed.

"Why don't you come along? Maybe if the town sees you with me, they'll get the idea you're helping me."

I hesitated. *Go with him? Out in public? Where people could see me?*

For a split second, doubt crept in—but it wasn't about my reputation. That ship had already sailed. This was about the case. If I wanted answers, I had to act like a detective, not a guilty librarian licking her wounds in the shadows.

And let's be real—I wanted to go.

I wanted to be in on this investigation, to have a front-row seat instead of waiting on the sidelines. I wanted to piece together the clues, feel that rush when something clicked into place. And maybe, just maybe, I wanted to spend a little more time with him.

But that was secondary. *Strictly secondary.*

I took a breath, squared my shoulders, and nodded. "Okay. Give me a minute to grab my messenger bag."

Time to get back to work.

That's what I told myself anyway. "Get back to work" apparently meant something entirely different to Brandon. It meant brooding silently as we drove to the lab instead of talking about the case.

When he entered the car after dropping the book jacket off at the lab, he said, "I ordered ahead so we don't have to wait."

Ordered ahead at The Tasty Burger. I didn't know there was such a thing. I smiled and thanked him, imagining grabbing a corner booth in the back where we could snuggle up and … really … talk about the case… and other things if they came up. By other things, I meant our relationship.

Before I could exit the vehicle at The Tasty Burger, Brandon opened his door and sprinted across the parking lot. Leaving me alone. With Agatha, who pawed at the window, clearly as confused as I was at this arrangement. The Tasty Burger was one of her happy places. They were famous for their doggie plates consisting of a tiny bunless burger and a few fries, followed by doggie-sized ice cream.

Three minutes later, Brandon was back, waving two brown paper bags, each closed with a sticker with The Tasty Burger Logo.

He opened the driver's side door and shoved a bag at me while addressing Agatha. "Dom says to tell you your regular order is in here?" He said it as a question, more for me than for her.

"They do a special doggy plate," I explained as I took the bag.

"Your car still at the library?" he asked, ignoring my

answer. Clearly he was in a hurry to get rid of me and keep working the case without me.

"Yes." Agatha pawed at the burger bag.

"I'll drop you there."

I didn't answer him and followed his tactic by addressing the puppy. "You'll have to wait till we get home girl."

In the five minutes it took to drive back to the library, Brandon and Agatha ate a batch of fries, him feeding her bits and pieces of each of his. She would be friends with him for life. She didn't seem to mind the lack of conversation about the case or anything else.

Brandon shoved the SUV in park in front of the library. Without turning off the engine, he hopped out and opened my door. My boots landed squarely in a mud puddle, my second mud bath of the day. Agatha refused to get out of the vehicle and leave her best french fry friend.

I reached in my messenger bag and pulled out her lead which, with much difficulty and a little wrestling a french fry bribe, snapped it on her harness.

Brandon set her on the driest portion of the pavement and she zipped across the mushy yard, dragging me along to the front door.

Brandon chuckled. "Catch up with you tomorrow," he shouted as a fresh burst of rain erupted from the sky. I scuttled to my car as fast as I could without saying goodbye.

———

That night I had haunting dreams of me wrestling with villains from Agatha Christie novels who turned into Brandon. I was puttering around my kitchen, making myself a cup of coffee when my phone buzzed.

Brittany:

Have you read my article yet?

I grabbed my iPad and opened my Maplewood Gazette news app and read the headline, subtitle, and first few paragraphs.

Copycat Killer Strikes Again: Agatha Christie-Inspired Murders Baffle Police—But the Sleuths Won't Rest Until They Solve It!

A Murder Fit for Christie—And a Killer Who's Still Out There

Janet's murder had all the hallmarks of a classic Agatha Christie whodunit—a locked-room mystery that left Detective Brandon grasping at straws. But when Ruthie's body was discovered in the town square gazebo, posed like a scene straight out of *The Body in the Library*, the unsettling truth became clear: a copycat killer is at work, and they're just getting started.

Gabby, the town's sharp-witted librarian, may have been arrested—but don't be fooled. It was all a ruse to get her inside the case. Now, she and The Sleuths are combing through every mystery novel in the library, hunting for clues that could crack the case. While the police play catch-up, they're already piecing together the killer's next move.

With a murderer taking inspiration from Christie's greatest works, the real question is—who's next?

CHAPTER 11

MURDER, MISDIRECTION, AND A VERY SUSPICIOUS LIBRARIAN

I DID my best not to ruminate on the worst-case scenario of the fallout from Brittany's article as I went through the motions of opening the library the next morning. I focused on the best-case scenario—patrons returning with their kiddos, apologizing and laughing about how they got it so terribly wrong the day before. I'd get back to work, helping them and conducting my beloved story hour and after-school program.

I shot Brittany a text.

> Thanks for being on my side and writing the article.

She answered:

> The old head librarian, Bea, ordered me to.

I replied:

> Yes, she told me.

She sent back:

> She scares me. Maybe she's the copycat killer.

The front door banged open as a gust of damp spring air swept through the library. Ned burst in first, his Sasquatch hoodie zipped up to his chin and rain boots squeaking with every step.

"We're here! Did Gabby get out of jail yet?" he yelled, dripping water and enthusiasm in equal measure.

Allison stepped in behind him, balancing a tote bag, an umbrella, and Roger's lunchbox. "Ned," she said calmly, guiding him forward with a hand on his back. "Remember what we said about *not* shouting about arrests in public spaces?"

Roger and Laura followed close behind, both blinking up at the high ceilings like they half-expected police tape to be strung between the bookshelves.

Laura looked up at Allison. "Is Miss Gabby still in trouble?"

"She's fine," Allison said gently, handing off a soggy umbrella to the coat rack. "And Mandy's not here today because she's helping her mom, not because of what happened yesterday. Okay?"

Ned leaned in with a dramatic stage whisper. "But *I*

think Gabby's gonna escape and hide in the woods like Sasquatch."

Allison shot him a look over her shoulder as she herded them toward the children's area. "You keep talking like that, and *you're* going to be the mystery story today."

Her face pinked as she looked me full in the face, then she dropped her diaper bag. "Mandy asked me to bring her kiddos, it's not because she…" She gathered the items that fell out of the diaper bag: wipes, snacks, and a few fidget toys.

Mary, set down the book for story hour, *And Then It's Spring,* and kneeled on the floor to help her. Once finished, Mary led the kids back to the story hour area while Allison continued to fiddle with her purse and diaper bag.

I stepped from behind the counter of the circulation desk. "Would you help me get the kids' snack ready?"

I knew she wanted to apologize but didn't know how. I didn't really care if she apologized, I was just happy things were getting back to normal and Brittany's article meant I wasn't branded a murderer.

In the small kitchen, I pulled strawberries and a bag of cheese cubes out of the mini fridge. Testing the forgiveness waters, I asked, "So are all of the kids going to be here today?" And quickly added, as I pointed to the plates she was arranging, "For the snack count."

"All except Fran's grandkids. They have a spring cold."

I sliced the top of a strawberry off and smiled. Everyone.

Allison arranged cheese cubes on plates as I

continued slicing strawberries. The main door chimed three times in a row, and the chatter of children's voices with an occasional "don't hit your brother." "Is that any way to act in the library?" and "good job taking off your coat, honey," drifted back like salve on a wound.

"You were here early." I dropped a handful of strawberries on a plate.

She dusted her hands off while Agatha searched the floor for cheese crumbs. "And you want to know why."

"Well, yes." I plopped the last handful of strawberries on the plate and removed my gloves, dropping them in the trash. With my back turned to her, I hoped it gave her time to think before she answered. Hopefully, she didn't say "I came to make sure you didn't have a stack of bodies in the back room."

Get a hold of yourself, Gabby, she wouldn't bring kids to check for a stack of bodies.

"Always the sleuth," she said as I turned to face her. "You will figure out who the copycat killer is. Won't you?"

I didn't want to say it wasn't a copycat killer. The truth was, we didn't know. Although Brittany's article painted me in a good light, by that I mean not a murderer, it still raised a lot of questions. And raised the fear level of the whole town.

She pulled her phone out of her pocket and shoved it toward me. "We have a group chat for the town's mom's group. It's nothing official or anything. Just a bunch of Moms."

A dancing monkey holding a straw moved across the screen. She quickly shut off the sound as Mary shushed the kiddos for the story reading.

"First you have brown, all around you have brown," Mary read.

The line floated out of the story hour circle, soft and simple, but it landed with a weight I hadn't expected. Brown, like the library carpet where I'd paced after being released. Brown, like the lukewarm coffee Detective Brandon offered me yesterday instead of an apology. I shifted on my feet and glanced at Allison—one of the only moms brave enough to show up today. Maybe spring was coming. Maybe this was just the part where everything looked dead, and you had to believe something was still happening underneath.

"I drew the short straw," she whispered. "It was my job to come early and text everyone if it was safe."

"You didn't really drop your diaper bag and purse," I whispered back.

"Girl, you are good! I was texting the group and I needed a…what do you call that?"

"A misdirect," I offered.

The rest of the conversation would have to wait. I thanked her and picked up a tray. The kids would be clamoring for snacks as soon as Mary read the last line.

After snack and craft time wound down—paper gardens drying on the windowsills, each one hiding a little seed packet with a scribbled wish or springtime secret—I watched the Moms slip into the fishbowl room, clutching coffee like it might hold the answers. The kids drifted to the Lego and activity tables, still smelling faintly of glue sticks and vanilla wafers, their voices rising in happy chaos while I tidied the edges of the morning.

Allison pulled out her phone again and read from the article.

"Okay, this part kills me," she said—then winced. "Poor choice of words. Anyway—'*Gabby, the town's sharp-witted librarian, may have been arrested—but don't be fooled. It was all a ruse to get her inside the case.*'" She laughed, shaking her head. "I'll admit it—I thought you *killed* someone for a hot second."

In the middle of our cozy coffee conversation, Detective Brandon stormed in, furious. "This just made my job ten times harder." He held a copy of the Maplewood Gazette and shook it over his head.

Agatha, excited to see her french fry best friend, yipped and darted like a spring rabbit who'd just unearthed a secret. When Brandon dropped the paper at his side, she grabbed it and yanked it out of his hand. She took a straight shot for her maroon-colored cushion in the corner.

I set my coffee down and put both hands on my hips. Emboldened by the pack of moms behind me, I retorted, "You didn't seem to care when you were dragging me to the police station."

He turned on his heel and strode quickly toward the door. With one hand on the handle, he turned and said loudly, "Stay out of this investigation, Gabby. Tell The Sleuths..."

Brandon didn't finish his sentence. He couldn't— James, Thomas, Antonio, and Randolph had created a complete bottleneck at the library entrance, talking over each other, waving newspapers, and generally making it impossible for anyone to get through. And, bringing up the rear, as if to add insult to injury, was Dr. Emory

Finch, the town's newest coroner, strolling in like he had all the time in the world.

Brandon stopped mid-sentence, his expression shifting from irritation to outright exasperation. He let out a loud, frustrated huff, glared at Emory and The Sleuths, then, to my utter disbelief, actually shook his fist at them like some kind of cartoon villain before storming out the door.

The library fell into a stunned silence. The kids at the Lego and activity tables froze, tiny hands gripping colorful blocks mid-construction. One particularly wide-eyed toddler, apparently unable to process the outburst any other way, toddled over toward us, wiped his nose on his sleeve, and promptly burst into a terrified wail.

Allison scooped him up with practiced ease, bouncing him lightly on her hip. "I think it's time we got out of here," she said. When I raised an eyebrow, she added, "Nap time," as an afterthought. The toddler's cries had quieted to sniffles, but the tension still hung thick in the air.

As she turned to go, she shot me a knowing look and nodded toward the SUV Brandon had climbed into. "Don't worry, we'll be back. *Me thinks he doth protest too much.*"

I blinked at her. "What?"

She just smirked and walked off, leaving me standing there, mouth hanging open like an idiot.

I joined The Sleuths in the fishbowl room. For the first few minutes, they didn't acknowledge my presence. They were too engaged in the newspaper article.

James, ever the dramatic, cleared his throat and read

aloud, his voice deep and deliberate. *"Each crime mirrors a Christie classic, meticulously staged, almost as if the killer is daring the town to solve the mystery before they strike again."* He exhaled, shaking his head. "I hate to say it, but this killer's got style."

Thomas scoffed, folding his paper with a snap. "Style? That's not the word I'd use. Here—listen to this." He smoothed out the page and pointed to a passage. *"The pattern is impossible to ignore. But Gabby and The Sleuths know that solving a literary puzzle in fiction is far different from stopping a murderer in real life."* He leaned back in his chair, arms crossed. "Well, at least it's not a serial killer targeting town council members. That's a relief."

I rolled my eyes. "Glad you're sleeping soundly, Thomas. Meanwhile, some of us are still wondering how many more bodies this copycat is planning to drop."

"Oh, hello, Gabby," Antonio waved his paper at me. "We are famous." He stood and waved at the Moms and kids exiting the library. "And the kids are back."

I couldn't help but grin. Antonio's joy was infectious.

James folded his newspaper and set it down, his gaze sharp. "So, my dear, let's solve this so you and your detective can make up. How about an espresso?"

I ignored the jab and crossed my arms. "We don't need caffeine—we need answers."

Thomas smirked. "And I think we know just the person to provide them."

Antonio tapped his fingers against the table, his

usual enthusiasm dimmed by something more calculating. "Owen Gallagher."

My breath hitched. "Owen? Why?"

James casually reached into his bag and pulled out a battered journal, its leather cover scuffed, the corners frayed. I recognized it instantly. He had promised me yesterday I could look at it.

My pulse kicked up. "Is that—?"

"The journal he left behind at book club," James said, flipping it open with a frown. "Supposedly notes for his novel, but it's mostly jumbled scribbles and scattered names. Nothing connects. If you ask me, it's either coded on purpose, or the ramblings of someone who's trying way too hard to sound clever."

Antonio let out a low whistle. "And guess what else is missing from the library's collection?"

Thomas drummed his fingers on the table. "The copy of *A Murder Is Announced*," he repeated what we already knew, but I was happy he didn't shame Antonio.

I inhaled sharply. "You think Owen took it?"

"What about Bea?" Antonio interjected. "She had the dust jacket."

No one acknowledged Antonio's theory. It couldn't be Bea. Why would a former librarian steal a book and then bring the dust jacket back? I shook my head. No. No. But there was the matter of her wiping the blood off the jacket.

James leaned forward, his voice barely above a murmur. "I think Owen's been plotting his own little Christie-inspired masterpiece. And I think it's time we asked him about it."

I swallowed hard. "Asked? Or cornered?"

Thomas grinned. "Depends on how guilty he looks when we 'invite' him to our next meeting of The Sleuths."

To this statement, Emory all but leaped out of his seat and yelled, "Best sleuths ever!"

I shushed him even though there was no need to since we were in the soundproof room.

"I suppose the conversation is a bit more stimulating here than in the morgue," Randolph elbowed him, and they both chuckled at their coroner joke. Looked like Thomas was relieved that the "bumping off town council people" idea was nixed.

James snapped the journal shut. "Let's hope he RSVPs. Otherwise..." He met my gaze. "We might be looking at the next victim."

CHAPTER 12
SUSPECT SPOTLIGHT

THE NEXT MORNING after story hour, The Sleuths and I gathered in the fishbowl room and waited for Owen. Would he show? Antonio had stopped and grabbed some fresh donuts. If we couldn't get Owen to talk, maybe we could bribe him with sugar.

Long and lean, Emory had eaten three donuts in five minutes, which filled him with more energy than a spring storm. He hopped around the room with Agatha and said things like "Isn't this fun?" and "We're going to interview a live one." At the last statement, he paused while Agatha seemed suspended in midair, snapping her jaw at the bit of donut he held. Emory grasped his belly and laughed at his own joke. Agatha took this opportunity to grab the last bite of the cake donut and gobble it down in one swallow.

It was in the midst of this crazy scene that Owen knocked on the door to the fishbowl room.

I opened it. He held his worn briefcase under one arm and held a mess of papers in the other. "I hope this is a short…" he paused and glared at Emory, who had frozen mid-laugh, "…and serious meeting. I have a book to write."

It was then that he spotted his journal on James' lap. Owens' eyes bugged out of his head. I expected him to say "hey that's my journal."

Instead, he walked over to the coffee bar and asked, "Are these donuts for everyone?" His voice squeaked like a mouse on the word "one."

He was acting guilty, but guilty about what? Murder? Stealing a book? Or both?

James stood and set the journal down on the chair while the rest of The Sleuths simply stared at Owen's back as he stacked half a dozen donuts on a plate. Bribery it is then. The leaning tower of donuts tottered and the top one fell onto the table. Agatha did another frog hop. I was fast enough to pop out of my chair and grab her in midair.

"You've had enough sugar." I took a quick glance at Emory, hoping he got the message too. He slumped forward in his chair, his elbows on his knees, as if he were about to watch his favorite murder mystery show.

I stepped out of the fishbowl room and carried Agatha to her maroon-colored pillow. When I set her down, she let out a contented sigh and curled up.

The library was buzzing with more patrons than usual. I'd spent the afternoon yesterday assuring regulars that I hadn't solved the murder and there was no proof that a copycat killer was on the loose.

Which was often followed by "but the paper said…"

Brittany, who'd yet to show her face at the library, had helped me, sure. But was she riding the high of the success of the article? I imagined her having Zoom interviews and packing her bags to move. All while I dealt with the fallout, including my ruined relationship with Brandon.

Bea interrupted my musing by tapping me on the shoulder as I filled Agatha's water bowel. I jumped, soaking my boots and the floor with water.

"See? I told you Brittany would listen to me, " she offered as I stood and went to the mini kitchen and grabbed a few paper towels.

"Thank you, Bea." I had a nagging question swimming around in my brain. I had to tread lightly. I mean, this was my mentor and my friend. If Brittany was leaving, I needed at least one woman friend. Janet was dead. The story hour moms were great, but they had busy lives and families to tend to.

My neighbor, Miranda, was great for an odd conversation, but she lived for her career. All of those thoughts swam around with the giant piranha of niggling doubt. The piranha won of course, and devoured all the other thoughts. My mystery mindset won out.

"It really is very dangerous to believe people. I never have for years."[1]

"Are you asking me where I was yesterday?" She froze.

"Yes, I am."

"That's private," she snapped as she grabbed the wet paper towels out of my hand and threw them in the trash can.

"Nothing's private when it comes to a murder investigation," I retorted with the same library-voice she'd just thrown at me.

"I suppose you are right. That detective of yours already questioned me about the book, you know."

"So much for me helping out with the investigation, " I said more to myself than her.

"Yes, he thought I was a suspect in the murders." She chuckled. "He thought I was the copycat killer."

We'd both made our way back to the fishbowl room without realizing it. Maybe I subconsciously led her that way so The Sleuths could question her with me.

"Before we go in there. I don't want everyone to know…" her shoulders slumped forward as she studied her sensible shoes. She shrugged and straightened back into her head librarian stance. She puckered her lips. "I'm dying, Gabby."

I swallowed hard. My throat felt as if it were closing up. I was choking with grief. My first thoughts should have been: *Is she in pain? What can I do?* Thoughts are not always the most unselfish things. My first thought was: she *is* leaving me.

"To answer your question, I was at the doctor yesterday in Grandview."

I wiped a few tears from my cheeks. "What did he say?"

"He said I have a few months left." She pulled a tissue out of her pocket. "Don't cry, Gabby. I've had a good life. I'm eighty-five years old. I'm ready to go."

I had my hand on the door of the fishbowl room. I was about to say all the things that people say: Is there nothing they can do? Have you gotten a second opinion?

She placed her hand on mine."I know how your

little Miss Marple Mystery brain works. No, I did not go on a killing spree in my final days on this earth."

Before I could correct her, Emory swung the door open and said, "Are you coming in? It's getting really good in here."

I sniffled and Bea took my elbow. "Yes, young man we are coming in, but has no one ever taught you not to interrupt?"

Emory stumbled back and caught himself on the back of a chair. "No… I mean I'm not good at social skills. I mean… I work with dead people all day."

Bea smiled. "Still got my head librarian skills," she said to me. "What is it you young people say? Chill out? I'm just teasing."

I took a few seconds to read the room. Owen clutched his precious journal while devouring a carrot cake donut. He no longer looked frightened or guilty.

"Are we finished?" I asked, sad that I'd missed everything, but glad I'd had a conversation with Bea. I could take her photo down from the murder board. It depended on what The Sleuths had found out whether I could remove Owen's name.

"They tried to steal my plotline for my bestselling novel." He shot James a withering look. "Guess James ran out of ideas. He had to steal mine."

James took a sip of his espresso, crossed his legs, and leaned forward with a dramatic pause in place, then continued, "I assure you my dear boy, I don't need your ideas. This town, and the copycat killer is enough fodder for a dozen novels. Especially if you are the next victim."

Owen clutched his journal tighter and shoved the

rest of the donut in his mouth. He stood, grabbed his briefcase, stuffed his journal, papers, and four more donuts in, then turned to address us. "Not if I write the bestseller first."

Which made no sense at all because in James' version, Owen was the next murder victim. He rushed out, pushing on the plexiglass door, smudging it with sugar glaze.

"Pull, dear," Bea said.

Owen turned sharply, his gaze cutting through us like a razor. His jaw clenched, his nostrils flaring as if he were biting back words. The overhead lights cast harsh angles on his face, sharpening the fury etched into every tense muscle.

Without another word, he yanked the door open, and the fishbowl room was instantly flooded with the hushed murmur of the library. The scent of old paper and fresh-brewed coffee curled around us, mixing with the distant rustle of turning pages and the soft clatter of a reshelving cart.

Heads turned. A few patrons froze mid-sentence, their curiosity palpable. A mother near the children's section paused, her toddler blinking up at the sudden movement. Mary, at the front desk halfway through stamping a book, hesitated, her eyes tracking Owen's brisk, furious departure.

Sunlight streamed in from the massive windows, catching on the dust motes that danced lazily in the still air. But Owen wasn't still—his steps were quick, clipped, echoing off the polished hardwood floor as he stormed toward the main doors. His long tattered army surplus coat flared behind him like a cape, the fabric rippling with the force of his stride.

As he reached the exit, he shoved the glass door open with more force than necessary, sending a rush of cool morning air swirling inside.

For a moment, the library remained frozen, like a book left open mid-chapter. Then, slowly, the whispers started—curious, cautious. The kind of hushed speculation that would soon ripple through town like an unraveling mystery.

James exhaled and leaned back in his chair, drumming his fingers on the table. "Well," he murmured, voice barely above a whisper. "Brittany did say the copycat killer had a flair for the dramatic."

A chill trickled down my spine. Because the way Owen had stormed out—angry, seething, and frayed—felt less like a man avoiding confrontation and more like someone about to snap.

CHAPTER 13
BESTSELLER OBSESSION

I STAYED LATE that night after the library closed. I pulled the murder board out and took a closer look at the murder suspects. On a table, I stacked the Agatha Christie books that I thought the copycat killer may be imitating. I copied a few quotes and plotlines on the board.

Whoever moved Ruthie's body must have wanted her to be publicly humiliated. Whereas Janet's body was left in her bed — a more private murder – as if someone didn't want her to be humiliated, just dead. I scratched my head. The only thing that made sense was a copycat murderer. Could it be Owen? He'd always seemed a little strange, but what would have set him off?

I grabbed a sharpie and wrote on the board under Owen's name.

No bestseller.

Was it possible that he was recreating murders from Agatha Christie novels in order to write his own bestseller? Knowing his favorite novel was *And Then There Were None* didn't make me feel any better. Was he knocking book club members off one at a time?

I stepped in the fishbowl room to brew a coffee and grab a leftover donut. Agatha yipped when I took a bite. "No more donuts for you. I'll grab you a doggie treat."

As I handed Agatha the treat and waited for my coffee to finish brewing, I found myself thinking about Owen. Always a little too eager during meetings, always steering the conversation back to the same book: *And Then There Were None.*

"We should read it next," he'd said more than once, his grin sharp, his eyes too bright. "It's the perfect mystery. Every detail, every death, executed with precision. Genius."

The usual groans and laughter had always followed. "We get it, Owen," someone had said. "You think Christie was the best."

He'd laughed it off, but I'd caught the flicker of frustration behind his smile.

Another time, he'd pushed further: "It's more than a great book. It's the blueprint for suspense. The ultimate locked-room mystery. A masterpiece of control. If a writer could pull something like that off in real life…"

He'd trailed off then, a dreamy sort of look on his face before shaking his head. "Well. Let's just say, that's the kind of story that gets remembered."

I shivered now, the words curling around me like a whisper.

"One of us in this very room is in fact the murderer."

Christie's line rang in my ears as I studied the board, my stomach tightening.

The thought had been gnawing at me for days. But here, alone in the dim library, it solidified into something heavier.

Owen had always wanted to write a bestseller.

And suddenly, I wasn't sure if he was trying to write one—or live one.

Agatha whined softly, nudging her damp nose against my hand. I exhaled and scratched behind her ears, forcing my pulse to steady.

I needed to figure this out before the book club ran out of members. I could be next.

A loud pounding on the front door caused me to jump and drop my donut into my mug of coffee. Maybe it was Owen. My phone buzzed. I set my donut-coffee on a table and pulled my phone out of my cardigan pocket, ready to bolt or call the police.

Brittany:

Let me in!

I breathed a heavy sigh of relief and jogged to the front of the library. I opened the door. "Brittany, you scared the —" I stopped short. Right behind Brittany stood Owen, grasping his briefcase.

I switched gears and put on my librarian voice. "Owen, the library is closed."

"Suit yourself," he said, turning on his heel and walking down the sidewalk.

"Wait," Brittany called, jogging after him. "You said you had something to tell us!"

"I'll be at The Tasty Burger if you want to talk, but the meals on you," he called over his shoulder.

Brittany jogged back to me. "Well, what are you waiting for? Let's go! Get Agatha."

There was no need to get Agatha. She'd joined us at the door and was furiously licking Brittany's shoes. I wanted to ask her why she'd abandoned me. Why she'd printed the article that had doomed my relationship with Brandon before it even had a chance to start, but this wasn't the time. Besides, what was there left to salvage anyway?

My feelings of abandonment took a backseat to having a late dinner with a serial-copycat-murder-mystery-killer.

I grabbed Agatha's lead and my jacket. I'd have to put the murder board away later. If Brittany was having dinner with a murderer, I wasn't letting her go alone.

The Tasty Burger was crowded. That was a good thing, unless Owen had a machine gun in his briefcase. *Get a hold of yourself, Gabby.* That's not the way Agatha Christie would murder someone.

Owen was scribbling in his journal. Maybe planning his next murder? Or writing a scene. Our scene. I imagined him writing:

Miss Gabrielle Keats, the town's studious librarian, smoothed a hand over the front of her high-necked blouse, her sharp blue eyes flicking toward the eager young reporter, Miss Brittany Lawson, whose ink-smudged fingers twitched with anticipation over her notepad. They sat in the dimly lit Crooked Candle. The scent of buttered rolls and roasted beef lingered in the air, while across from them, Mr. Owen Gallagher—tall, lean, and always just a touch

disheveled, as if he'd stepped away from his desk mid-thought—scribbled furiously in his journal before glancing up with a sly grin. *"You must admit, ladies,"* **he said, his voice smooth yet edged with something almost conspiratorial,** *"there is a certain poetry to an unsolved crime."*

Owen noticed us and gave us a lazy wave and went back to scribbling in his journal. When we joined him and slid into the booth, he simply said, "I'll take the number five with the works."

Our waitress joined us, grinning from ear to ear at Agatha, whose body was shaking in anticipation of her doggy dinner.

"Your regular?" she said as she reached over and scratched Agatha behind the ears.

"No," Owen said without looking up. "These ladies have my order and they are paying."

She frowned and pulled her order pad out of her apron pocket. "I wasn't talking to you, Owen," Then added, "What will it be ladies?"

I smiled and tapped the plastic-covered menu."I think you know what Agatha wants." I ordered Owen's food and then my own. Brittany followed suit.

Once our waitress left, Brittany pulled out her phone and said, "Okay, Owen, spill the beans."

"Not until I get payment. By that I mean, my dinner."

"That wasn't the deal," Brittany said. "You planned to tell Gabby what you'd learned at the library earlier."

Brittany had told me in the car on the way over that she had found Owen in the alley between the library and bakery, loitering. When she had spotted him under a street lamp, he had explained he was getting up his nerve to come in and talk to me.

In turn, I'd filled her in on my theory of Owen being the Agatha Christie copycat killer. I'd reminded her of the conversations at book club.

"Owen?" she'd replied dryly. "He's a bit strange. But knock people off so he can write a bestseller about it?"

Brittany now took a long noisy slurp of her iced tea. "Gabby here thinks you're the Agatha Christie copycat killer."

Two scenes unfolded simultaneously. Detective Brandon entered The Tasty Burger with Officer Greg, and I choked on the lemon water I was sipping, which startled Owen.

"That's right," Brittany continued. "We called the police."

Owen slammed his journal shut and sputtered, "I didn't … I'm not…" He stood. And then sat down with a hard plop.

Detective Brandon and Officer Greg strode across the restaurant to our table. I dabbed at my blouse with a napkin where the water was making a lovely heart-shaped stain with a jagged crease in the middle.

Owned seized his journal and shoved it in his brief-case. "I'm leaving." He stood and scooted out of the booth, red-faced. He yelled, " Flo, I'll take my order to go."

"Not so fast, young man." Detective Brandon blocked his exit.

Owen froze and squeaked, "Am I under arrest?"

Detective Brandon stood with his hands on his hips, fingering the clasp over his gun. "Have you committed a crime?"

"I…" is all Owen said.

He pulled his phone out and waved it in front of Owen's face. "Because I got a text a little bit ago about you."

Owen glared at me.

I held my hands up in surrender. "It wasn't me."

"It was me," Brittany said. "Why don't you sit back down, Owen, and tell us what you were going to tell Gabby?"

Owen squatted to sit, missed the booth seat, and fell on his butt. Detective Brandon reached down and pulled him up and then winked at Brittany.

He winked at Brittany? Were these two in cahoots? Brittany, seeking the one article that would get her the dream job. Brandon, leaving me out after he'd asked me to help, so he could take credit for solving the Agatha Christie copycat killer case. And Owen, who they thought was an eccentric wanna-be bestseller was bumping off bookclub members right under their noses.

I grabbed Agatha and pushed on Brittany's hip with mine. "Scoot over and let me out. I'm leaving."

She moved slowly, probably hoping I'd change my mind. "Don't you want to know what Owen has to tell us?"

I shoved her hard the last three inches and slipped out. Agatha whimpered. I may have squeezed her too tightly, or maybe she thought she wasn't getting her doggy dinner.

I patted Agatha on the head reassuringly. "You'll get

your dinner." And then I turned to address Brandon and Brittany. "I'm not playing whatever this game is."

I walked to the counter and told them I'd pay the bill and take my food to go. I sat on a stool at the counter and waited, feeling Brittany and Brandon staring at me. When I turned to look, I found my feeling was wrong. They were chatting. *Chatting*. And Owen was gone.

I took Agatha and our take-out order and fled the restaurant. Brittany would have to get her own ride. I had one hand on the handle of my VW bug when someone tapped me on the back. I jumped and Agatha growled. I fully expected it to be Brandon, coming out to correct me.

"It's just me, Gabby. No need to be afraid."

"Owen."

"I'm not telling them what I found out. I told Brittany I wanted to tell you and you only."

"Really?" I croaked.

"Yeah. Can I get a ride?"

CHAPTER 14
THE CONFRONTATION

"LET'S GO SOMEWHERE PRIVATE," Owen said as he slid into the passenger seat.

"What do you mean, private?" Every Miss Marple-like sleuth bone in my body was screaming at me not to go anywhere private with Owen, the copycat killer. Wasn't the point of his obsession with *And Then There Were None* that everyone died? I could imagine the scene he'd write about my death:

Miss Gabrielle Keats, the town's devoted librarian and amateur sleuth, had been remarkably easy to lead astray. A woman of intellect, yes—but like all those who fancied themselves detectives, she suffered from the fatal flaw of believing she was always one step ahead. She fancied herself a Miss Marple, but in the end, she was just another eager moth drawn to the flame of a well-spun lie.

A promise of information, a whisper of intrigue, and she willingly slid behind the wheel, hands steady,

heart racing for all the wrong reasons. How simple it had been. How tragically predictable. As the headlights cut through the thick night, the weight of inevitability pressed in, but she never saw it—never suspected that the very story she so desperately wanted would be the last one she'd ever chase.

"Why alone?" I croaked.

"Oh, I mean not in front of Brittany and Detective Brandon." I agreed with him. My anger and embarrassment fueled what might be the most deadly decision of my life.

I didn't want to take Owen to my house. The library seemed the most obvious choice. So back to the library we went. Once inside, Owen hightailed it for the fishbowl room while I served Agatha her doggy dinner.

I set my messenger bag on the circulation desk and slid my phone in my pocket in case I needed to call someone. Who would I call? Not Brittany. Not Detective Brandon. I quickly texted James.

> AT LIBRARY WITH OWEN. POSSIBLY DEAD BY THE TIME YOU READ THIS. DON'T CALL POLICE

I knew the text didn't make any sense. Why shouldn't he call the police? And dead...wasn't that taking it a little too far?

The three dots danced across the screen for an eternity.

Finally, he texted back:

> On My Way

I swallowed, squared my shoulders, and walked toward the fishbowl room like I knew what I was doing. On the outside, I looked composed. On the inside, my stomach was a pit of burning lava.

"Mind if I have a few more donuts?" Owen said as he stuffed five leftover donuts in his briefcase in quick succession.

"Sure."

He eyed my The Tasty Burger takeout bag. "Are you going to eat that?"

I shoved the bag toward him and he squished it and stuffed it in his briefcase. With my best Miss Marple voice I asked, "Owen, what did you want to tell me?"

He hesitated. I didn't know if he was going to kill me now or ask for more food. He eyed the coffee maker.

"How about I make us some coffee and we can chat?" The words were out before I could stop them. Now I had to turn my back—give him the perfect target—and pretend I wasn't terrified.

"While I make the coffee, could you check on Agatha?"

"Can I give her a fry?"

"Absolutely," I said with more force than I should have. What were my choices at this point? An over-stuffed, spoiled puppy or a dead me. Who was I kidding? Agatha was already a spoiled puppy. The fact that she would take a fry or two from a killer was concerning, but if it would save my life, so be it.

He left the fishbowl room, whistling and calling, "Agatha."

I loaded the coffee filter with grounds and pushed the button. When Owen didn't return right away, I took the opportunity to pull his journal out of his briefcase. I was going to die anyway. I'd like to at least know why.

I thumbed through the journal and found a plethora of laboriously copied quotes from *And Then There Were None*. James had briefly shown me a few of the plot ideas Owen had jotted down.

If anything, it was more confusing now—just a jumble of half-baked thoughts. Maybe the illegible notes of a madman. Or maybe just someone who couldn't figure out how to write a novel.

I shouldn't have opened the journal.

The second Owen stepped into the fishbowl room, I knew. He hadn't expected me to see it—his real hand-writing: the raw, unedited mess of his mind spilled across the pages. He hesitated in the doorway, fingers curled around the handle, before forcing a smirk.

"Gabby," he said, low and lazy, but there was some-thing tight in his voice too. "Didn't take you for the type to pry."

I closed the journal carefully, but I didn't let go of it. I wasn't done yet. "Didn't take you for the type to be afraid of a little help."

His sneer flickered. Just for a second. Then he stepped inside, letting the door swing shut behind him. The library's glass-walled fishbowl room suddenly felt smaller.

He sat across from me, fingers tapping a slow rhythm on the table. "You think I need help?"

I glanced down at the pages, still warm from where my hands had held them open. The ideas—*brilliant* ones—were all there. Twisted, dark, fascinating. But so were the signs. Words crammed together, others stretched apart like he'd lost track of where they should sit on the page. Letters flipped. Spelling inconsistencies that weren't laziness, but something deeper.

"You wouldn't let James Hatterson help you," I said. "Not because you don't want help, but because you don't think you deserve it."

His jaw tightened. "And what makes you think that?"

I shrugged. "Because you're dyslexic, Owen."

Silence. The kind that drops heavy between two people when something true has been spoken out loud. His fingers stopped tapping.

I folded my hands over the journal, watching him. "Agatha Christie was dyslexic. So was F. Scott Fitzgerald. Even Stephen J. Cannell—he created *The Rockford Files*, *21 Jump Street*—wrote over *450* scripts and still struggled with spelling. You think they let that stop them?"

Owen exhaled slowly, shaking his head like he was amused, but I saw the tension in his shoulders. "And you think that's what this is? Some sad little self-esteem issue?"

I lifted the journal slightly. "I think this is you, proving to yourself you can write. Even if you won't admit it."

His fingers twitched. His expression smoothed into something unreadable. "And what if I said you were right?"

I smiled. "Then I'd say stop getting in your own way."

He studied me for a long moment, then leaned back in his chair. "You're interesting, Gabby."

I huffed a quiet laugh. "And you're predictable." I tapped the journal. Part of what I'd imagined at The Tasty Burger, he'd actually written at some point. "I read this entry of yours—the one where you describe how easy it was to lure *her* away." My fingers curled around the edges of the leather cover, my voice steady. "How simple it was. How she *thought* she was a step ahead. That's what you wrote, right?"

Owen didn't move. Didn't blink.

"She wanted the truth so badly, she didn't even see it coming." I lifted my chin, meeting his gaze dead-on. "You're talking about me, aren't you?"

A slow grin stretched across his face, something dark flickering behind his eyes.

"See, Gabby," he murmured. "You really are clever."

The air in the room shifted, and for the first time, I knew—I *really* knew—this was a story I might not get to finish.

My phone buzzed, interrupting our conversation. James:

I'm here. Let me in!

"James is here. I'm going to let him in," I stated with more bravado than I felt. My hand shook as I put it on the handle.

He saw the tremors and stood up. "Is this an intervention?"

I stepped back and let him open the door, wondering if I'd gotten it horribly wrong.

"I thought this was a murder scene."

He stumbled back. "What... I would never..."

"Why did you want to come here alone with me?" I knew I should go let James in, but I wanted to know.

"Brittany has ulterior motives. So does Detective Brandon." He stepped back to let me pass. "I think you don't and you're the only one who can solve this case."

"So tell me."

"Janet's son, Brett, stole *A Murder Is Announced*. I saw him sneak into book club, grab a cranberry and white chocolate cookie."

"What does taking a cookie have to do with the book?"

"Bea told me there was a red residue on the cover."

"Cranberries."

"Exactly. And the idiot discarded the dust jacket in the alley."

"How do you..." My phone buzzed again, followed directly by sirens wailing up the street.

He backed away from me. "You called the police?"

"Of course not. I'm not talking to..."

I stopped myself. That sounded ridiculous. I'm not talking to the head detective, so I barricaded myself in the library with the man I thought was the copycat killer.

The sirens stopped and blue and red lights flashed.

"I'm going to run out the back," Owen said.

For a brief moment, I hesitated, the weight of the moment pressing against my ribs like a held breath. Brandon was outside, his voice sharp through the megaphone, demanding Owen step out. His mind was already made up—he thought he had the killer. But they were wrong.

"Owen Gallagher come out with your hands up!" a loudspeaker squeaked.

"What should I do?"

"Go with the police. Tell them what you told me."

I met his gaze, steady and sure. "Owen, burying your demons in a journal won't erase them. And running?" I shook my head. "That only makes you look guilty. You're not. So go out there, answer their questions, and prove it."

"What if they shoot me?"

"I'll walk you out and explain that you are not the killer."

He picked up his briefcase and hugged it to his chest.

I linked elbows with him and led him to the front before he could change his mind.

CHAPTER 15
THE AFTERMATH

OWEN SHOVED me in front of him as we exited the library. A spotlight blinded me and I tripped over Agatha. I righted myself. It took me two seconds to realize it wasn't a spotlight, but the flash of a camera.

I froze with my hands up in surrender just like in the movies. Owen stayed behind me.

"Owen is coming willingly in peace." I was going to add "don't shoot," but that would feed Owen's fears and he might turn and run back into the library. Which would make him seem guilty.

Owen stepped out from behind me. "I'm not the Agatha Christie copycat killer."

Detective Brandon and Brittany moved toward us in a synchronized motion. Brittany snapped photos while Brandon snapped handcuffs on Owen.

"Really, Brittany?" I said with disgust. Then I realized my hands were still held up in the surrender position. I was pretty one hundred percent positive that some version of my mouth hanging open and hands in the air would appear in the paper tomorrow morning.

"Am I free to go?" I asked them both.

I was tempted to tell them that Owen wasn't the killer, because, well, he wasn't. But at the same time, I wanted them to crash and burn. I wanted Brittany to print the article and not get the job. I wanted Detective Brandon to fail.

"Yes," Brandon said, rather offhandedly, as if I weren't the victim of a hostage situation and didn't warrant further questioning. Or at least a check by an EMT.

James joined me after hiding behind Brandon's SUV for the entirety of the exchange.

"My dear, shouldn't we go inside?" He took me by the elbow.

I turned, and with my hand on the door to the library, I had second thoughts and third thoughts. I watched while Officer Greg guided Owen into the back of the police cruiser.

"Aren't you going to say anything?" Owen yelled.

"What's going on?" Cora shouted from across the street.

Brittany paused her photo-taking spree to turn and shout back, "We caught the Agatha Christie copycat killer is what is going on." She snapped a few more photos before continuing, "Read all about it in the Maplewood Gazette tomorrow."

Cora looked both ways on the empty street before jogging across on her stylish heels. James was pulling on my elbow, trying to get me to go into the building. But my second and third thoughts kept me frozen in my tracks. I envisioned Brittany losing her job to the young intern for printing another article that required a retraction. I envisioned Brandon losing his job, and our relationship dissolving as he moved back to the big city to take another job.

Cora stopped and peered into the cruiser before joining us.

James reached a pleading hand toward her. "Cora, my dear, will you tell Gabby to come inside?" He held the door open and waved his hand in a forward motion.

"Oh, Owen."She let out a soft sigh, the kind reserved for kids who should've known better but didn't. "Of course. Let's get you inside, Gabby."

"She was just held hostage by that wanna-be-a-best-selling-author," James explained.

"Oh my. Isn't his favorite book *And Then There Were None*?"

"Very perceptive of you," James said, as I let myself be led into the library and back to the fishbowl room. "We think he is bumping off the book club members one by one so he can write a book about it."

"Oh my," Cora exclaimed. "How awful."

I hadn't said a word. I was too busy wrestling with my second and third thoughts. And probably suffering a little post-traumatic I-was-just-a-hostage-but-not-really disorder. I sat down heavily and Agatha comforted me by licking my boots.

"She's in shock," James stated. "I'll make her a double espresso with double sugar."

"What can I do to help?"

"I guess we can disassemble the murder board.

Maybe that will make Gabby feel a little better." James pointed outside the room. "It's right there."

"I see. Like she might snap out of it if she realizes she solved the case and the killer is behind bars."

Cora, polished in a tailored blazer and sleek heels that somehow made no sound on the library floor, complied with a nod and exited the room.

"It's not solved James," I said.

The espresso machine hissed and he didn't hear what I said. I jumped up as Cora wheeled the board into the fishbowl room. Cora paused to study the board. James finished my drink and plopped two sugar cubes in it.

"Sit down and drink this, my dear." James shoved me back into the chair. I took the cup and swished it down my throat in two swigs. "Satisfied?"

"That should perk you up in a minute." He smiled and patted me on the head as if I were a small child.

I gritted my teeth and whispered, "Owen didn't do it."

His eyebrows knit together into two angry fuzzy caterpillars. "Why didn't you tell the police that?"

"Believe me, I tried. Detective Brandon and Brittany have their own theories and don't want my input."

In a quick nutshell, I shared the night's events at The Tasty Burger and how Owen and I ended up here alone.

"So what you're saying is, you let a could-be copycat killer in your car and drove him here. Then you proceeded to come in the library after hours with him alone."

"That about sums it up," I answered.

Cora rejoined us. "Want me to take all the photos down for you, Gabby?"

James crossed his legs and leaned back in his chair. He puckered his lips and then asked, "Have you been listening to what Miss Marple did this evening?"

Cora stood beside the murder board, one hand still on the frame like she was ready to wheel it right back out. "I heard some of it. Gabby, you could have gotten yourself killed."

She leaned over and patted me on the leg—gentle, measured. But something in her face didn't match the words. Not shock. Not worry. Just the faintest flicker of relief, smoothed over too quickly.

Agatha took the gesture as a sign that Cora's shoes needed a good licking – Agatha's love language.

"But he didn't harm me or have any intention to," I answered.

"Did you tell the police that?" Cora asked.

"I asked her the same thing. Apparently the handsome detective and Brittany have their own theories and don't want to hear what Miss Marple here has to say."

What had Detective Brandon said earlier? *"This just made my job ten times harder."* He had shaken a copy of the Maplewood Gazette over his head. This morning he had not been in cahoots with Brittany. What changed? What did she know that we didn't? What did he know that we didn't?

"Can you make me another one of those?" I asked James as I stood.

Agatha had finished giving Cora's shoes a thorough cleaning and promptly fell asleep. Poor thing. She was probably traumatized and exhausted from the evening as well.

James smiled. "Another double shot it is. And maybe the three of us can figure out who the real copycat killer is."

I let Agatha sleep while Cora and I studied the murder board.

I glanced toward the espresso machine, hissing like a steam engine. "Oh, James, you can't hear me, can you?"

No answer—just the steady hiss of the machine.

"You can tell me if you like," Cora said, lowering her voice, "and I'll fill him in while you sip your drink."

"Oh, okay." I pointed to Brett's photo—Janet's son. "He stole the copy of *A Murder Is Announced* and tossed the dust jacket in the alley."

"I heard he had money troubles," Cora said, staring at his photo like she could will it to confess. "Do you think he killed his mother and these cases aren't connected at all?"

"That's where some of the facts are leading." I uncapped a marker and paused, the tip hovering over the board.

Curiosity isn't just about wanting answers. It's what drives you to keep asking questions—even when the answers start to hurt.

I scribbled what Owen had told me beside Brett's name:

Snuck into book club the night the book went missing—stole a cookie.

Then I chuckled.

"What's so funny?" Cora asked.

"Well, Bea found the dust jacket in the alley and cleaned it with a disinfecting wipe."

Cora's eyes grew wide but she laughed as well. "Sounds like Bea. Everything orderly and clean." Then she added, as an afterthought, "Was there any evidence on it?"

"That's the funny part. It had smudges of red, according to Bea. I thought it was blood."

She leaned forward as if I were delivering key evidence to the police. "It wasn't?"

"Remember, we had cranberry white chocolate cookies during book club. Owen saw Brett sneak in and grab one."

"And he took the book," James concluded, "while we were busy chatting."

James joined us, and soon we were laughing at ourselves—cranberry smears mistaken for blood. But that's the thing about solving a crime. The world tilts, and suddenly every budding branch casts a suspicious shadow, every casual remark seems laced with hidden meaning. Even every book club member, with their dog-eared paperbacks and bottomless cups of coffee, seems capable of harboring a secret—or at the very least, a perfectly crafted alibi. And no one—not even Bea, the retired librarian with her perfectly alphabetized flower beds—is above suspicion.

James handed me the double espresso. Then he turned to Cora. "Here you go, Cora. I believe flat white latte is your poison."

Cora recoiled for half a second before taking it. "Thank you. Forgive my reaction, but coffee this late…"

"I took the liberty of adding a swirl of caramel on top."

Cora thanked him and took a quick sip.

"Oh, I need to tell Brittany." I picked up my phone and texted her.

Owen isn't guilty. Whatever you're planning on writing about, don't.

I set my phone down. As much as I wanted to call or text Detective Brandon, I was going to do what he asked me to.

"Back to the investigation." I picked up my coffee and took a sip. "Where's Agatha?"

James turned and took the ten steps back to the fishbowl room and peeked in. "She's still in the fishbowl room, asleep."

"Today must have really worn her out," I said.

Cora studied the board. "This is both exciting and scary."

"I agree. I don't think Brett killed his mother. So that puts us back at square one for the murderer."

"But what you said about the facts."

"Yes, my dear, but facts aren't the only things we rely on."

"I don't understand," Cora replied.

"What he means is, we must have motive. And why would he kill his mother, the one he doted on and shared coffee with at her house every morning?"

"Janet was such a sweet woman." Cora wiped a tear from her eye. "Sorry, I'm not cut out for murder investigations. I spent my life solving my kids' disputes. But this is a different kind of horrible."

"Of course, my dear," James said. "It is a great deal to handle. And if I remember correctly, Janet helped you on occasion with those kids."

Cora sniffled and set down her coffee mug, which read "Murder, She Sipped."

"It must have been quite a blow for you to lose Janet."

"Yes, it was. And I thought when the police arrested Owen…" She took a shuddering breath. "I thought it was over and Janet got justice."

"And Ruthie," I added.

"Of course. And Ruthie. Of course, I didn't know her as well."

Cora reached for her oversized satchel—soft caramel leather with brass hardware, stylish without trying too hard. It was the kind of bag that looked like it belonged in a catalog photo, right next to a matching planner and an herbal tea sampler.

As she grabbed the handle, it tipped forward and three candles spilled onto the library floor, rolling gently against the base of the murder board.

I smiled without thinking. "Oh—more candles?"

Each was wrapped in Cora's signature way: a layer of soft tissue paper tied with twine, a tiny pressed flower tucked under the knot. Lavender, peach, and one plain white—unscented and a little heavier than the others.

"Oh the candles!" I exclaimed.

Cora froze mid-squat, her knees crackled in protest. "What about the candles?"

"I love mine so much. I've been burning it every night."

"Oh." She straightened and put a hand on her lower back, which creaked as she popped it back into alignment. "I'm so glad."

"Could I have one for the library?"

"We could put it in the fishbowl room," James added. "It does get rather stuffy in there."

"That's a nice way of saying that The Sleuths sometimes let off a certain odor." I giggled and placed my hand over my mouth like a third-grade girl. I was feeling better about the whole investigation. Not that I'd figured anything out. But I *was* relieved that Owen wasn't a murderer, just a young guy with a reading disability. Although Brittany and Brandon seemed to be in cahoots, it couldn't dim the fragile relief of simply talking about candles and not crime scenes.

I reached down and grabbed a sage green one before she even said yes. "Can I have this one?"

"Well, I…"

"Of course, Cora wants to share, don't you my darling?"

The "my darling" did her in. She blushed and brushed a strand of hair out of her eye. She shook her head in the affirmative.

"Let me grab your coat and I'll put this in the fishbowl room."

"Promise me one thing," Cora said quickly. "Don't use it tonight? But here, Gabby, take this one for your house." She thrust a lavender candle into my free hand. "You're welcome to burn it as soon as you get home."

I hugged the lavender candle she'd handed me.

"We'll save the sage green one for when all The Sleuths are here, so they can enjoy it together."

I set the sage candle down in the fishbowl room and glanced at Agatha. Still dead to the world. "Sorry, girl. Today was a little much for you, wasn't it"

I delivered Cora's coat to her and she left after James helped her put it on and placed her satchel on her shoulder.

As the door closed behind her, James said, "I think that's all we can do tonight. I'll put the murder board away."

"Yes, I agree. I'll clean the coffee machine and straighten up the fishbowl room."

With his hand on the board, he asked, "Are you okay? Really? I mean, Owen kidnapped you."

"No, I misread the situation."

"That's not like you."

"That's true. My instincts told me something was off with Owen."

"We all knew that."

"Don't judge him too harshly. It's not what you think. I'd like to talk to you about him and explain everything. Just not tonight."

He nodded his head and smiled. I began to clean the coffee maker while James wheeled the murder board back to the hallway. He joined me as I finished and wiped the coffee counter down.

I scooped Agatha up. James, always the gentleman, walked me to my car.

He shut my door. I started the car, gave him the thumbs up sign and watched him walk to his car.

Once back home, I expected Agatha to wake up. But

she didn't stir, so I carried her in and placed her in her bed.

After consuming two double shots, added to the nerves brought on by my pseudo-kidnapping, I couldn't sleep. I picked up an Agatha Christie short story, *The Thumb Mark of St. Peter*, and read for a few minutes before hopping up to grab a plate full of cookies.

Normally when I would pull a vintage floral plate out of the cabinet, it would bring Agatha out of a deep sleep in half a second. I opened a container of cookies and peered behind me so I didn't trip on her when she sprung up, begging for a bite.

But this time, she didn't spring up behind me.I set the plate down and went to check on her. Still asleep. I panicked and checked for a heartbeat. It was there. Slow, but still ticking.

Then a horrific thought crossed my mind. *She's been drugged*. I shook her. No response. I did the first thing that came to mind: I ran to the kitchen, grabbed my phone off the counter and punched a button.

Before she could answer, I said, "Brittany, Agatha's been drugged. The only person who fed her tonight was Owen. He gave her a french fry."

She didn't hesitate. "I'll pick you up in five and we'll take her to the vet."

Yes, of course. The vet. At this point, it didn't matter who poisoned her. What mattered was keeping her alive.

When we arrived at the vet, Brittany opened my door for me. With tears streaming down my face, I ran inside, saying to myself, *you can't leave me, Agatha. Everyone leaves.*

CHAPTER 16
A NEAR DEATH EXPERIENCE

BRITTANY EXPLAINED to the nurse on duty that Agatha had been poisoned, because I couldn't speak. A nurse with the name Velma stitched on her scrubs top took the wet-rag puppy out of my arms and whisked her back to the vet on call.

I tried to follow. Brittany pulled me back. "Let them do their job." She gently led me to a seat and pushed my shoulders so I would sit.

"She can't die. How could I have been so stupid?"

Brittany stroked the copper tangled mess of my hair. "You're not stupid."

"Owen asked me if he could give her a fry and I let him. All the while, he *is* the Agatha Christie copycat killer." I dropped my head in my hands and wept without restraint. Shudders shook my frame as the toll of the last few days hit me.

Brittany rubbed my back and let me cry without correcting me or asking questions.

Ten minutes later, nurse Velma said over the

speaker, "Gabby Keats." As if there were a room full of pet parents.

"We're the only ones here," Brittany said under her breath as we jogged to the front desk.

"Gabby," nurse Velma said while glancing back and forth between us.

"That's her." Brittany pointed. I don't think the nurse had any deduction skills. My face, I'm sure, was red, swollen, and blotchy from crying.

"Dr. Vance says to let you know the puppy will be fine. He pumped her stomach." She shoved a form at me.

"So I can take her home?"

"No, we need to keep her here for observation. Just sign this and give us a credit card to pay the charges."

I pulled a credit card out of my messenger bag. "Can I see her?"

"No. Absolutely not."

"Now I know why this nurse is not on day shift. She's got the people skills of a rock," Brittany whispered.

"What was that?" the nurse responded as she zipped my card through a machine.

"I said we need the contents of Agatha's stomach."

"Let's chat about that." The vet stepped up from behind us, and I jumped like Agatha did when I got the cookies out.

"Sorry to startle you. I'm Dr. Vance." He lightly touched my elbow. "Let's take a seat."

We returned to our seats in the waiting room, and he took the seat opposite me. "Your golden doodle had an interesting array of food in her stomach."

"Yes, she loves food."

"People food. Like fries. Donut. Hamburger."

"So you're saying she couldn't wake up because she ate too much *people food* as you call it," Brittany said, ever the reporter.

He straightened the lapel of his lab coat. "Oh. Well. No. As a vet, I'm saying in the future, don't allow her to eat so much of it."

Brittany stood and shook a forefinger at him."But you aren't Agatha's vet. You're some random vet. Probably not a great one if you're doing the graveyard shift."

"It's okay, Brittany. Sit down. He's right. She does eat too much people food." I pulled on her jacket but she didn't budge.

Brittany stepped back an inch and put her hands on her hips. "Again, are you saying Agatha went into some sort of food coma?"

"No, I'm just offering some advice."

"We're going to need whatever you pumped out of her stomach."

He stood and faced her nose to nose. "Are you questioning my ability as a vet?"

I jumped up and squeezed between them. "Of course she isn't. Thank you for your advice and for taking care of Agatha."

Dr. Vance relaxed his shoulders and un-balled his fists.

"This is part of a police investigation," I explained.

"We think someone poisoned ..."

Dr. Vance straightened his collar and pushed his glasses up the bridge of his nose. "The dog? But why?"

"Because he was going to kill her next," Brittany pointed at me. There was a clatter and a shriek at the front desk from Miss-no-personality nurse.

Brittany turned to me. "Get Dr. Emory on the phone and tell him we have Agatha's stomach contents for him to test."

"Dr. Emory Finch, the new coroner?" Dr. Vance sat back down. "What's going on around here?"

Brittany looked offended now. "Yes. Haven't you read the papers? There's a copycat killer running around recreating murders from Agatha Christie novels."

A large thump resounded from behind the front desk.

Brittany ran and peered over the front desk. "I think your nurse fainted."

"I'll tend to her," I offered. "You go get whatever you pumped out of Agatha's stomach."

Dr. Vance rushed back the way he'd come in, and within thirty seconds reappeared with a plastic container labeled "golden doodle stomach contents."

"I took the liberty of calling 911 for your nurse," Brittany said as she grabbed the container.

We didn't leave until Dr. Vance let me take a peek at Agatha, who was sleeping soundly. I breathed a sigh of relief as I patted her. "I'll come and get you first thing in the morning. Thank you for not dying."

I called Dr. Emory from the car. "You want me to what?"

"You have a problem with testing dog puke?"

"Of course not. I'm happy to help. It's just my first canine subject."

"She's not dead," I said.

"Of course not. I'm sorry. I'm not used to dealing with live bodies."

Nor does he have any social skills.

"You're on speaker," I added. "Brittany is here."

"The correct thing to say is 'I'm so sorry your puppy was poisoned.'"

"Well, we don't *really* know that," Emory explained. "We'll have to run some tests…"

"We're hanging up now," Brittany said.

Brittany clicked the end button. "The world is full of people who have no social skills."

I gave her a quick sideways glance. "Speaking of people with no social skills."

She shot me a confused look, her eyebrows arching in a flying geese V. "What?"

"Why are you in cahoots with Detective Brandon?" Now that I knew Agatha was going to be fine, it was time to deal with the case of the best friend gone rogue.

"What?"

"Don't act like you don't know what I'm talking about. The Tasty Burger. You and Detective Brandon."

"Yes?"

"You called him?" I didn't mention the wink. I wanted to hear what she had to say first.

"Yes, I called him. I felt bad that my article got you in trouble with him."

"Got me in trouble? He's not my…"

"Your boyfriend."

"I was going to say dad." But I didn't know how a dad acted when his daughter was in trouble, I thought to myself.

"Sure," she said as she shifted in her seat and switched gears. "No, really, I felt bad. I had a plan. I called Brandon and apologized and invited him to The Tasty Burger to meet us."

"And?"

"And then I was going to leave you two lovebirds to work it out." She flicked on her blinker, its steady click ticking along with our conversation, then turned onto my street. The streetlights hovered like lazy fireflies in the fog, their glow stretching and shifting as if unsure where to land—much like our conversation, drifting between confusion and clarity.

"So it wasn't about getting the scoop to write your next article?" I asked as she pulled in my driveway and put the Supersonic Red Toyota in park.

The overhead light clicked on and I looked her full in the face, searching for truth.

She hunched her shoulders and blew out a heavy blast of air. "Okay. Okay. You got me. It wasn't at first…"

"But then Owen had something to tell me and…"

"I couldn't resist," she said, finishing my sentence. "Aren't you proud of me?"

I opened my door and stepped out onto the wet pavement. A light mist was falling. "Proud of you for what?"

"I haven't asked you what he told you."

She rounded the front corner of the SUV and jingled her keys.

I stopped for a second. "Yes. I am. You didn't once bring it up on the way to the vet or while we were there."

She put an arm around me. "Yeah, well we thought Agatha… and you were crying your eyes out."

"Let's go inside and I'll tell you everything Owen said," I offered.

"Mind if I spend the night? It's two in the morning." She let go of me and skipped up to the porch without waiting for my response.

Once inside, I loaned her a pair of PJs. I grabbed us both a water bottle and the plate of cookies I'd left on the countertop. I switched on the gas fireplace and we settled in front of it, like college co-eds staying up for a late-night gossip session.

I took a bite of a peanut butter cookie and, with a mouthful of cookie, said, "Wait, what story are you running tomorrow?" It sounded more like, "wa , wuh soree u run trmr?"

"Good thing I speak Gabby-has-a mouthful." It was a joke that her mom, Sally, had started when I went to their house after school for the first time. I'd gotten so excited about fresh baked goods, I had spoken with my mouth full. Well, that and I'd had no manners or social skills at the time. Really, I couldn't help myself at the time. I had been beside myself to be included in a real-life after-school snack-and-chat with a family.

"Gabby-has-a-mouthful" had stuck. Of course, I'd had to play it up because Brittany's mom thought it was so cute.

"I don't have an article tomorrow. Boss gave it to the intern. Said I'd gotten too much into sensationalism."

"By that, you mean Detective Brandon called the paper and complained." I shoved another cookie in my mouth and chewed while I thought. And yet, she was willing to put her goals aside and reach out to Brandon for my sake.

"You believe what I wrote, don't you?"

"That there is a copycat killer?"

"I do now. I can't believe I fell for Owen's poor-me shtick."

"Owen has lived on the fringe of society for so long, it's not hard to believe that he fell off the edge."

"He poisoned my dog!"

"You were next."

"You can print that."

"If I'm ever allowed to write another article."

"What's the intern writing about?"

She hopped up. "Let me grab my laptop. I was supposed to edit it before it goes to press."

I sipped my water and stretched my legs out in front of me.

Brittany plopped down on the sheepskin beside me. "Listen to this:

'The Sky is Sweating and the Oceans Are Angry: Climate Change is Here

The weather isn't just weird—it's downright moody. One minute, record-breaking heat waves; the next, torrential floods washing out entire towns. Scientists blame carbon emissions, but politicians bicker while nature throws tantrums. Farmers are confused, coastal towns are bracing for the worst, and somewhere, a polar bear is definitely not thrilled. Whether it's too late to fix it or not, one thing is clear: climate change isn't coming—it's already banging on the door.'"

"Is she for real? I thought you were supposed to edit that?"

"Boss said only for grammar and spelling so that's what I did. Apparently we are supposed to write everything at a fifth grade level."

Brittany groaned and flopped against the couch. "It's a *disaster*." She took a furious bite of her cookie, as if sheer force could will the article into something respectable. "I told her to focus on *facts*. I told her to keep it neutral, to report news, not some weird *climate change fever dream*. And she just nodded at me like I was a background character in her life and then *wrote that*."

I hid my grin behind another sip of water. "Well … she's got passion."

Brittany let out a strangled laugh. "She's got *delusions*." She waved the cookie in the air. "The boss says we write for a fifth-grade reading level. But this? This doesn't sound like she *passed* fifth grade."

I plucked a cookie off the plate and took a bite, chewing slowly. "Some people have to figure things out the hard way."

She groaned and slumped forward, arms on her knees. "Yeah, well, she's about to get *educated* when the mayor's office calls to complain." She tossed the laptop onto the couch and shook her head. "I don't get it. If she'd just let me help…"

I tilted my head. "Like Owen?"

Her eyes narrowed. "What about Owen?"

I set my glass down and leaned back in my chair. "You keep pushing him to let James Hatterson help with his novel, but you don't get why he won't take the advice."

Brittany crossed her arms. "That's different."

"Not really." I took another sip of water. "Owen has dyslexia."

The words landed between us like an unseen weight. Brittany frowned, her mouth opening slightly before snapping shut again.

"He never said—"

"He doesn't talk about it." I shrugged. "He's always had to work twice as hard just to keep up, and now he's finally trying to do something on his own. Handing his words over to someone like James? That probably feels like putting his brain on display and inviting the world to critique it."

Brittany exhaled and picked up another cookie, turning it over in her hands. "I thought he was just being stubborn."

"Oh, he *is*," I said, grinning. "But not for the reason you thought."

She let out a breath, shaking her head. "That actually explains a lot."

I grabbed another cookie and leaned back. "It usually does."

"I guess he'll be writing the bestseller from prison."

She shoved her face into a pillow and screamed. When she came up for air, she said, "I'm going to lose my job to a third grader."

"No, you are not. Can I ask you a question?"

She threw the pillow aside. "Shoot."

"Do you usually *edit* her articles more?" I put an emphasis on the word "edit."

"You mean fix them to be factually correct and at

college level? Of course I do. I want people to respect the paper."

"Well, I'm glad you didn't this time. It's time for Miss High-and-mighty to fall off the pedestal the editor has placed her on."

Brittany's phone buzzed on the coffee table, rattling against the wood. She grabbed it, glanced at the screen, and sighed. "It's Emory."

I perked up. "Dr. Finch? Why is the coroner calling *you*?" Instead of me. My mind instantly jumped to the worst-case scenario. Agatha was going to die.

She gave me a look before swiping to answer. "What's up, Emory? I'm putting you on speaker. I'm at Gabby's house."

"Oh, hi Gabby. I didn't think you'd want to wait until morning for the results."

His voice came through, calm but edged with something I couldn't quite place. "I got the lab results back."

My stomach tightened. I sat up, setting my water down carefully.

"For what?" Brittany asked.

"The stomach contents from Agatha."

My breath caught. Agatha—my dog, my shadow, my constant companion—had almost died.

Brittany went rigid beside me. "And?"

Emory hesitated, just for a second. Long enough for my breath to catch.

"There was arsenic in her system."

The room didn't spin so much as tilt—like my brain was trying to tip the world back into place and failing.

Arsenic.

Someone had poisoned my dog.

Brittany's phone slipped in her grip, screen glowing against her palm. "You're saying—"

"I'm saying it wasn't an accident," Emory said, voice tight and clinical. "Someone tried to kill her."

A cold chill crept up the back of my neck, slow and certain. Agatha—my snack-loving, couch-hogging, fry-stealing sidekick. Someone had looked at her and made a choice.

I tightened my fingers around the armrest, grounding myself. "Then I know who did it."

CHAPTER 17
CASE SOLVED?

"AT LEAST OWEN is already behind bars," Brittany said as she patted me on the shoulder.

I sat on the couch and hugged my knees to my chest. "I thought he was telling me the truth. That he just wanted to tell me Brett was innocent."

"He took advantage of you, kidnapped you, and as I said, you were probably next."

"I'm just glad Agatha is okay," I said as a tear slipped down my cheek.

"I think it's time we turn in. You've had quite the day."

I rose like a girl in a trance and walked to the bathroom to brush my teeth, counting the hours until I could pick Agatha up in the morning.

Brittany joined me and nudged me with her hip. From the medicine cabinet she pulled out the toothbrush she kept here just for nights like these. Not exactly nights like these. Because although I'd had a difficult childhood which meant a difficult transition into adulthood, I'd never been kidnapped by an Agatha Christie copycat killer. My dog had never been poisoned.

I spit out the peppermint toothpaste and reached for the mouth rinse. I swirled the tingly mint around my cheeks, which puffed out like a chipmunk full of acorns. As I spat, I wondered—had Agatha Christie ever poisoned a dog in one of her novels? Probably not. Even murder had its boundaries.

"Race you to the bed!" Brittany teased as she ran the floss through her front teeth.

I knew she was trying to distract me and cheer me up at the same time. It wasn't working. My brain was in gear.

"What if Brett didn't take the book, *A Murder is Announced*, from book club Monday night?"

Brittany took a swig of the wash and swirled it around before spitting. "What?"

"No dog is poisoned in *And Then There Were None*."

Brittany grabbed a hairband and pulled her hair into a messy bun. "Again. What?"

I grabbed the face wash and lathered up my face. "Owen is going off-book, so to speak."

She took the face wash from me and smeared it on her face in circular motions. "So?"

"That's not like him. He's very … what's the word…linear."

"You mean how he's been trying to write the same bestseller for years."

I handed her a washcloth. "Yes. Despite his difficulties, he's never veered from the course."

"Until today, when he kidnapped you and fed an arsenic-flavored french fry to your dog."

"I'm suddenly not tired," I said while I splashed water over my face. My speech was garbled, but Brittany understood and shook her head in agreement.

She shook her lavender-scented washcloth at me, splattering my t-shirt and the mirror. "Want to help me write my next article?"

"I'd love to." I splashed a handful of water at her.

After our brief water battle, we settled in my small library room off the kitchen. She grabbed her laptop while I pulled some Agatha Christie novels off the shelves.

"*Dumb Witness* has a dog. It's a Poirot mystery. The dog isn't poisoned though."

Brittany paused her furious tapping on the computer keys and suggested, "You've got to get it out of your head that Owen wouldn't go off-book, as you call it."

"What have you got so far?"

Mystery Writer Turned Suspect: Owen Gallagher Arrested After Poisoning and Hostage Standoff

Maplewood's growing unease over the so-called Agatha Christie Copycat Killer reached a boiling point last night when local mystery writer Owen Gallagher was arrested after allegedly holding Gabriella "Gabby" Keats against her will in her own library. In a shocking turn, Keats's beloved dog was poisoned and is currently under veterinary care. While Gallagher's connection to the copycat killings remains unconfirmed, his disturbing actions have

**sent ripples through the community, leaving many
to wonder—was he just another obsessed writer, or
something far more sinister?**

"I can't let you print that," I said, arms crossed as
Brittany's fingers danced over her laptop keyboard.

She didn't even look up. "I can print that Owen
Gallagher was arrested. That's a fact."

"Yes, but you're calling him the copycat killer, and
we don't know that yet." I motion to the empty dog bed
in the corner, the blanket still rumpled from when I
carried my dog out the door. "He poisoned my dog, he
held me at the library, I think. I didn't try to leave. But
that doesn't mean he's responsible for the murders."

Brittany let out a slow sigh, arms crossed tight
across her chest. "Gabby, he writes mystery novels, he
was obsessed with the case, and he literally trapped you
in the library. If it looks like a villain and acts like a
villain—"

"Then maybe it's just a desperate writer who got in
over his head," I said, the words coming out low and
clipped. "And maybe, if we're not careful, we're going
to lock up the wrong person just because it's
convenient."

She leaned back in her chair, arms folded. "I'll keep
it factual. Owen Gallagher was arrested. Your dog was
poisoned. You were held hostage. All true."

I exhaled and rubbed a hand over my face. "Just...
don't make him the copycat before the cops do."

Brittany hesitated, fingers poised over the keyboard.
"Fine. But if it turns out I was right, I'm giving myself
an 'I told you so' column."

I shook my head, exhaustion settling deep in my bones. "You do that." I snapped the murder mystery shut and added, "I'm going to bed."

"You're not mad again are you?"

"No. Just tired."

"Okay. I hate when you're mad at me."

I paused in the doorway and gave her a quick smile. "Thank you for that. Oh, how are you going to get that printed in the paper tomorrow?"

"Oh the paper has already gone to bed, it will be in the online edition if I can get ahold of my editor."

I snuggled under the covers and dreamed of Agatha and murders I'd read about in books. My dreams were short-lived. Two hours later, my alarm went off and I tumbled out of bed, excited to pick up Agatha from the vet's office.

I grabbed my pink and blue plaid robe and slipped it on.

"Brittany?"

I walked toward the kitchen and peeked into the library. No Brittany. I searched the rest of the house. I found a note in the typewriter.

"Boss said 'yes' to the story. Going live at 8 am. See ya later! Love you."

I must have been really out if I hadn't heard her plunking away on the ancient keys.

Oh well. According to her, the case was solved. Owen was behind bars, and I was going to pick up Agatha. It was going to be a great day.

CHAPTER 18
NOT SO HAPPY ENDING

I UNLOCKED the library while juggling Agatha's leash, my messenger bag, and a bag of donuts. Agatha's vigor had not been dampened by her near-death experience last night. Nor did she agree with the doctor that she should alter her diet. Cake donuts were one of her favorite treats. She rocketed, twisting her leash around my legs. I stumbled through the door and hit the floor, but managed to keep the donuts from smashing by thrusting them into the air with one arm.

"Let me help you," Brandon said from behind me.

Why did he always find me in the most embarrassing positions? It didn't matter. He could see me twisted up on the floor right now for all I cared. I was just happy the case was solved and Agatha was okay. Nothing could dampen my mood. Not even the dark storm clouds threatening on the horizon line. But I was still mad at him.

I huffed and said, "Take the donuts while I untangle myself from Agatha."

That wasn't the best choice. He took the donuts and Agatha lunged for him, wrapping me tighter in her leash, my legs immovable. I scooted forward like a wriggling worm, fresh out of the mud. When the door closed behind me, I opened the clasp on Agatha's leash and freed her. She bounded after Brandon, who'd taken the donuts to the fishbowl room.

I laid there for a moment. Panting. Unable to move. I had a quick thought – why hadn't Owen tied me up? I dismissed it just as quickly. Nope. Don't Gabby. Owen poisoned your dog for goodness sake.

I rolled across the floor until my legs were free. I stood and hung the leash up on a hook by the door and brushed the dirt off my plaid pants.

Brandon was leaning up against the doorway of the fishbowl room, eating a cinnamon cake donut and feeding bits of it to Agatha. "She really got you, didn't she."

"Agatha?" I wasn't sure if he was referring to Brittany and his little scheme yesterday, or the world's most embarrassing entrance a few minutes ago.

"Yes. If I need help apprehending a suspect, I'll borrow her." He took another bite of the donut and dusted his hands on his jeans.

"I think Agatha's days of being in the crosshairs of criminals are over." I walked past him and flipped on the espresso machine.

"Yes. Of course," he said, straightening and pulling down his sweater.

Forgetting for the moment how angry I was at him, I switched gears and asked, "Not going into work today?"

He shook his head. "Taking the morning off."

Then, like he couldn't help himself, he added, "You like the sweater?" He brushed a few donut crumbs off the periwinkle knit like it hadn't been chosen with great care.

Agatha licked a few more crumbs off his freshly polished boots.

"Nice boots," I said, trying not to sound surprised. They looked like something out of a catalog—*rugged but emotionally available*. I didn't even know Brandon owned shoes that weren't regulation.

And the sweater? The cologne? He could pretend he'd just wandered in for a casual visit, but the outfit told another story. He'd gotten dressed for someone.

I just wasn't sure if he realized it was me.

"Are they giving you the morning off because the Agatha Christie copycat killer is behind bars?" I continued as I pressed the espresso with a tamper.

He plopped into a leather chair and interlaced his finger on his chest. "Am I being interrogated?"

"No. I just... well... I..." I flipped the switch and the hiss of the machine saved me from finishing my sentence.

"I came to apologize," he said when the machine stopped. I poured the shot into a tiny cup that read "Espresso Yourself," then knocked the wet grounds out. The loud pounding gave me a chance to think about how I was going to respond.

"You yelled at me in front of The Sleuths and my library patrons."

"I know. I know." He hung his head and grasped it in both hands.

"And you and my best friend conspired behind my back."

He looked up sharply. "It wasn't like that. I had a problem with *her*, not you. I never meant for you to get caught in the middle."

"Yet you took it out on me. You know, Miss Marple always said people show you who they are by how they behave when no one's looking. Or in your case—when everyone is."

He stood and took my espresso cup and set it down. He took my elbows. "I'm sorry for all of it, really. For arresting you. For conspiring, as you call it, with Brittany."

I looked into his eyes. He was sincere. Those steel gray eyes. Eyes I could swim in and never be tired of ...

I pulled back.

"You're not getting off that easy." I picked my espresso back up and took a swig.

"I didn't think I would. That's why I came to ask you to dinner. So we could talk things out."

"Oh." The heat rose from my toes to my nose. No doubt my freckles glowed like little blinking lights, saying yes, of course.

Instead of answering, I said, "Did you read Brittany's article?"

"I did and you can tell her thank you."

"Why don't you tell her?"

"Oh no." He held his hands up in surrender. "I'm not going there again."

He pulled his phone out and scrolled before clicking on the article. "I appreciate that she said: 'While Gallagher's connection to the copycat killings remains unconfirmed, his disturbing actions have sent ripples through the community, leaving many to wonder—was he just another obsessed writer, or something far more sinister?'"

"Yes, I told her she couldn't just report as a fact that Owen was the copycat killer."

"I thought her article had more of a Miss Marple flair." He chuckled. He slipped his phone back in his pocket and crossed his arms as he leaned against the coffee counter. "So is that a yes to dinner?"

"On one condition."

He leaned toward me, his face close enough to mine to give him a kiss.

"You come to The Sleuth's meeting today and publicly apologize to all of them."

He leaned back as if I'd burned him. "What?"

"Those are my terms." I filled the coffee carafe up with water to make a regular pot for the staff and story hour moms. "I'm doing you a favor, you know."

"By making me apologize?"

"Yes. This is how small towns operate. We may not always get along, but we apologize when we mess up."

He fumbled with a coffee mug.

"You might want to try a 'yes sandwich.'"

"A what?"

"Thank you for helping me solve the case. I shouldn't have yelled at you. I'd appreciate your help in the future."

Brandon had grabbed a napkin and scribbled furiously.

"Are you writing that down?"

He glanced up for a microsecond. "I'm not good at apologizing."

"I wouldn't say that."

He paused. "Can you say that last sentence… wait, why wouldn't you say that?"

I pressed the button on the coffee maker and it hummed to life, pushing the fragrant brew into the pot.

"Well, you came like that…" I waved my hand over his outfit. The jeans, the periwinkle sweater, and those eyes.

"Those eyes are part of me all the time."

"Oh, did I say that part out loud?" I averted my gaze. Don't look at the eyes. My boots. Look at my boots. For a millisecond, I thought about Agatha's habit of licking shoes for clues. I shrugged it off. "I meant you made an effort." It was then that I noticed his sweater matched my plaid pants.

The door chimed, ending our moment, or whatever this was.

"Yes to your terms." He gave me a quick peck on the cheek and turned on his heel to go. "Text you later," he called over his shoulder.

"I could sleep for a week," Brittany said, pausing in the doorway just long enough to be noticed before striding in and grabbing a donut.

"Those are for my staff and the story hour moms," I teased.

"If that's true, why is there one missing? It's Saturday. You don't usually have story hour."

"I ate it," I lied. "I decided to try a Saturday morning story hour once a month for the working moms."

"I bet the handsome detective who just kissed you had a donut."

With a fresh donut available, as well as a new pair of shoes to lick, Agatha left her pillow to beg.

"No, Agatha, you've had enough."

"Oh so she already had some donut crumbs." She took a generous bite of her donut and then grabbed a coffee cup. "Please." She held it out to me while grinning from ear to ear.

"What are you so happy about? It can't be my dinner date with Brandon."

Brittany jumped up and down. "You have a date with Brandon. So my plan worked?" She squealed and did her signature happy shoulder shimmy, a quick little wiggle like her joy couldn't quite stay put and had to escape through her collarbones.

"Not exactly." I handed her a cup of coffee. "But the wording in your online article today helped."

She sipped her coffee. "The article you helped me write."

"There's something you aren't telling me and you'd better speak quickly. The story hour kiddos will be here in ten minutes."

"Well, the article you helped me write got me in good with the boss again."

"There's more," I said, holding my breath. Did she get the big city job? Did I just help her leave me?

"He fired the intern."

"What does that mean?"

"I'm not losing my job."

I grabbed her arms, and her coffee sloshed on the

floor. She set it on the counter and we danced a hoedown around the room.

She stopped to catch her breath. "Yeah, I just met with the boss, and when he found out I'd been writing her articles, he confronted her."

"What did she say?"

"She still thinks her work is something worthy of a literary award." She bowled over laughing. "And that's not all. The Grandview Herald editor, Hank Remington called me and…"

She didn't get to finish as a horde of kiddos and moms descended on the fishbowl room with gifts for Agatha—dog toys, squeaky bones, and enough treats to fill a kiddie pool.

Allison led the charge. "We heard what happened. And, of course, read your wonderful article, Brittany." She handed Agatha a plush squeaky taco. "The other moms and I raided the pet store as soon as it opened."

Agatha took the taco and bolted, tail wagging like a metronome on triple time. A chorus of giggles followed as she trotted proudly out of the fishbowl room, kids trailing behind her like she was leading a parade.

"Wait for me, Agatha!" Ned shouted, already halfway across the library. "I brought her the *Sasquatch squeaky*! It makes the noise *only* wild dogs can hear!"

They snaked through the library, circling a puzzled patron near the mystery shelves, and disappeared back into the kids' area.

I'd have to finish my conversation with Brittany later. I needed to get back there before Agatha led story hour.

Story hour was a success—by my standards, anyway. What I mean by "successful" is Agatha was the star, and the kids were just happy she was okay after her night at the vet. They all wanted a dog book, so I swapped the planned title for *Three Names* by Patricia MacLachlan. We made it to page ten. Agatha loved every second of the attention. She was the star and she knew it.

With story hour wrapped up and a peaceful hush settling over the library, I set out fresh donuts and straightened the chairs in the fishbowl room, getting ready for The Sleuths.

Agatha slept on her maroon cushion, worn out by the attention and activity of the morning. I had moved her cushion into the fishbowl room so I could keep an eye on her. The vet had promised there should be no more effects from the drug, but I didn't want to take any chances.

James rushed into the fishbowl room, his spicy cologne leading the way. "My dear, what an ordeal you had last night."

"I am so glad you weren't the next victim of the copycat killer," Antonio said, coming in a close second and adding the fragrant smell of basil to the spice. He paused and leaned over to pat Agatha on the head, his substantial pizza dough-like belly folding over his belt. "You too, girl."

"And that's a wrap," Thomas announced as he straightened his bow tie. "The Sleuths solve another crime."

Thomas had been exceptionally jolly since we'd determined there wasn't a serial killer bumping off the town council.

Dr. Emory and Randolph brought up the rear. Emory rubbed his eyes and yawned. We'd both had a long night. "Let me get you a coffee, Emory."

He smiled and quietly said, "Thanks."

I poured him a generous mug full of coffee and handed it to him."Thanks for running the test for Agatha in the middle of the night."

He gratefully accepted the mug and slurped half of it down in a few gulps. "Of course."

Randolph handed Emory a plate with two donuts. "We're all grateful," he added.

Allison stuck her head in the door. "Did I miss anything?"

Story hour was over. Hadn't she left with the other moms?

"Oh, the other moms asked me to come back and get the full scoop on… well… everything."

There'd been a few comments during story hour about Brittany's article *Mystery Writer Turned Suspect*, but they were whispered and in three-second increments.

Allison grabbed a mug and poured herself a cup of coffee. The slogan wrapped around the ceramic in vintage typewriter font-"Shhh… someone in this room is probably a murderer."

"So first off, the moms want to know, are we safe? Like is the Agatha Christie copycat killer in jail?"

I blinked and wondered where this version of Allison had been hiding. I mean, she'd always been one of the leaders in the moms group — great at organizing, helping out, and watching other moms' kids. But this Allison. She was so poised, in control, and seemed to have a list of questions to ask us. Like Brittany.

"Well, to answer your question," I said as I handed her a donut. "Owen Gallagher, like Brittany's article reported, is locked up for the murders."

She accepted the donut and took a small nibble. "But we don't know if he is the real copycat killer."

"He poisoned Agatha with a french fry." Antonio crinkled his eyes shut and answered as if that explained everything. "Only an Agatha Christie copycat killer would poison a dog with a french fry."

"Allison, did you have a career before you had children?"

Allison typed something on her note app. "I'm asking the questions here."

I pointed and said one word, "Journalist."

"Of course you would figure it out. Aren't you the one who broke this case wide open?"

"If by that you mean got in the car with a murderer and brought him to the library, then yes."

"Mind if I join?"

"Simone, my dear," James said. "Please come in."

"I'm not your dear. Don't try that fancy talk with me." She blushed. I wasn't buying the mean school marm act for one second.

"I wondered if you were discussing the case?" Simone squeezed past Antonio and took a seat next to Thomas.

Randolph and Emory had moved to seats next to

each other and were deep in a conversation about the case.

Randolph leaned back in his chair, watching Emory with the kind of knowing look that only came with decades of seeing the worst humanity had to offer. "You look like something the morgue dragged in, kid."

Emory let out a tired laugh. "Appreciate that. Just pulled the biggest case of my career out of the morgue, so you know… sleep's been optional."

Randolph shrugged. "Biggest case *so far.* Stick around long enough, you realize there's always another body waiting in the wings."

"Comforting." Emory traced the rim of his coffee cup with his thumb.

"Not my job to comfort you," Randolph said. "My job was to retire and let you deal with all this mess."

Emory leaned forward, lowering his voice. "It wasn't some big Sherlock moment. More like… I just stopped thinking like an investigator and started thinking like him. Every murder followed an Agatha Christie plot, but then—"

I chuckled. Emory thought he'd solved the case. Brittany thought she'd done the same. So did Brandon. Let them all. I couldn't help but add, "—but then he went off script."

"Exactly," Emory said. "Agatha. It wasn't a clean Christie-style death. It was rushed. Sloppy. That's when I knew he was losing control."

Randolph nodded. "Amateurs always do. The fantasy of being a killer is always neater than the reality. Blood doesn't pool the way they expect. People don't die on cue."

If by going off-book he meant killing—or attempting to kill—a dog, then Emory was right. That wasn't in the script.

Agatha Christie adored dogs. Her own beloved terrier, Peter, was so dear to her that she dedicated *Dumb Witness* to him. He trotted through her life, as faithful as any literary companion, and even made his way into her fiction, though never as a victim. Christie could spin tales of betrayal, poisonings, and well-plotted revenge, but she never murdered a dog. That was a line she never crossed.

Miss Marple would say that people reveal themselves in the details. A change in habit, an alteration in pattern—those were the real clues. A man meticulous enough to recreate crime scenes from literature would hardly abandon his chosen template so haphazardly.

So, what had changed?

Miss Marple would sip her tea, settle into her chair, and let her knitting needles click while she worked it through. A person's true nature, she would say, always comes out in the end. The killer was one kind of man before, and quite another in the end.

Which meant—either Emory was right, and the copycat lost his nerve, lost control, lost his grand plan… or someone else had killed Janet and Ruthie.

I turned to Simone. "What do you think?"

"About the murderers or who was murdered?"

Allison continued to type on her notes app while we chatted.

"Either," she answered for me.

"Janet was the sweetest lady. I don't know why

anyone would want to kill her, Agatha Christie-style or not."

"And Ruthie?" I asked.

Simone huffed. "Most wicked woman on the face of the earth."

"Explain," Allison said as she held up her phone. It was then that I realized we were part of the moms' zoom meeting. The moms' faces lined up in squares like the Brady Bunch kids, a show I'd watched in one of my many foster homes.

"Gabby knows. I don't like to talk about it. I can't tell you how many times I wished that woman was dead."

I wished she hadn't said that. The Zoom meeting was being recorded. If it turned out Owen was innocent of killing Janet and Ruthie, which it probably was, then Simone would look guilty of Ruthie's murder.

Allison paused and held the phone up to my face while she and six other moms waited for me to explain.

I took a breath and scanned the room. All eyes were on me.

Antonio dunked his donut into his coffee, oblivious to the shift in the room. "I just don't get it. Why wouldn't Simone like Ruthie? She was nice enough."

Across from me, Simone sat still, hands resting on the table, her fingers lightly curled around her cup. She didn't flinch, didn't jump in, didn't rush to correct the assumption.

I swallowed a sip of coffee, keeping my voice calm, deliberate. "They had history. One with consequences."

Allison frowned. "What kind of consequences?"

Simone didn't answer, so I did. "Simone lost her job

because of Ruthie. She led the charge to have her removed from the school after an alleged incident with a student. It wasn't just a job—she lost her pension, her reputation, her career." I paused, then added, "Ruthie didn't believe in letting obstacles stand in her way."

Simone exhaled softly, but otherwise remained quiet.

Thomas, arms crossed, made a gruff sound. "Oh, come on. It wasn't just Ruthie. The board had concerns. The community had concerns."

Simone lifted an eyebrow, finally looking at him. "The *entire* community?"

He set his cup down with a little too much force. "There were reasons."

"That doesn't mean they were good ones," I said calmly. "Or true."

The silence stretched.

"I suppose that's the question, then," Simone said, voice even. "Was justice served—or simply decided?"

One of the moms on Zoom cleared her throat. "So, you're saying Simone had a *reason* to dislike Ruthie?"

"I'm saying," I replied, "that Simone lost everything she had built for herself, and Ruthie was the one who made sure of it."

Simone let out a soft hum. "It reminds me of *Five Little Pigs*."

Allison blinked. "What?"

"The Agatha Christie novel," I said.

Simone inclined her head slightly. "A woman is convicted of murder. The case is closed. The matter is settled. And yet, years later, the details begin to shift, and the truth comes out—she wasn't guilty after all."

The silence that followed was longer this time.

Thomas pushed back from the table. "I think I've heard enough."

Simone's lips curled in the faintest hint of a smile. "I imagine you have."

He stood, straightened his shirt, and walked out of the room without looking back.

Allison exhaled and took a long sip of coffee. "Well. That was tense."

On Zoom, one of the moms shifted in her seat. "This murder case gives me chills."

I looked at Simone, who was finishing the last of her coffee with quiet, steady patience.

Miss Marple would say that people rarely see themselves as villains. That when they tell their side of things, they always believe they are the wronged party.

And yet, Miss Marple would also say that *the truth has a way of finding the light, no matter how long it's been buried.*

CHAPTER 19
BURIED TRUTH

SIMONE LEFT IN A HUFF. I get it. She felt misunderstood and as if she were the victim. I thought she was, but few people did. Sure, she was a tough teacher, but fair. She expected us to do our work. Ruthie hadn't liked to do the work to get the grade. She expected to sail through on her looks and took shortcuts.

Brittany and Allison left soon after, both juggling the kind of real-life responsibilities that didn't pause for murder investigations. Allison had kids to wrangle and a grocery run to make before picking up her other kids at a friends, and Brittany muttered something about needing a nap and a reset before her next article.

The Sleuths were packing up to go to lunch, and Detective Brandon hadn't showed yet. Maybe he didn't want to go out to dinner.

"Mind if I join you for lunch?" I asked James.

"Of course not, my dear."

"Are you sure you're up to it?" Thomas asked.

"Yes. Then I'm going to go home and take a short nap. Let me just go talk to Mary."

"Count us out," Randolph said as he pointed to himself and then Emory. "I want to check Agatha's sample and review the postmortem on Janet and Ruthie."

"He wants to make sure I didn't miss anything," Emory explained as he stifled a yawn.

"Yes, since Emory caught the killer, you'll need to make sure he didn't miss any clues," I said.

The joke sailed over Emory's head and into the atmosphere. Randolph gave me a quick wink.

"Sorry I'm so late gentlemen," Detective Brandon said as he stuck his head in the fishbowl room.

"And what exactly are you late for, Detective?" James said as he straightened his collar.

I hadn't told The Sleuths about my deal. An apology to them for a dinner date. Now that I said it to myself, it sounded ridiculous. What if he wasn't sorry and he just wanted to pump me for more information? No. That couldn't be.

Brandon had changed into his detective attire. So I was right. He'd shown up here in the jeans and sweater and the eyes on purpose. To charm me. *Stop it Miss Marple me.* This isn't 1950 . He's not trying to charm you or be swoon worthy. Whatever he wasn't trying to do, he was doing it.

Antonio shoved a glass of water into my hand. "Please sit down Gabby. You're all flushed. I'm afraid you are coming down with something."

James turned and looked me full in the face. "She's

coming down with something all right." Then he turned back to Brandon and glared.

"I need your help. There have been some developments in the case."

I took a sip of my water and cleared my throat loudly.

He shifted his position and put both hands on his hips. "Oh right. I'm sorry, Sleuths, for not respecting you and chastising you in public."

"Chastising us?" James shot me a look. "Seems like someone put you up to this apology. Miss Marple."

I stood and set my water down. "Yes, I did. He asked me out to dinner and I said not unless he apologized."

"Did you also write the apology speech?" Thomas smiled. He was used to someone writing speeches for him, so I'm sure it wouldn't surprise him.

I took another gulp of water and swallowed before answering. "No … I may have made some suggestions but I didn't write it."

"We accept your apology and dinner proposal," James said, and offered his hand.

Detective Brandon gave a swift, hearty shake and then added, "So will you help me?"

"Of course," I answered for the group. "Emory and Randolph are off to the morgue to recheck Emory's findings."

"But the rest of us would be happy to take you to The Tasty Burger and you can brief us on the case." James plopped his fedora onto his head—because of course he owned one—and waved an arm toward the door as we filed out of the fishbowl room behind him.

I rode with James, Antonio, and Thomas. James's 1985 Mercedes-Benz 300D idled at the curb, its deep emerald paint catching the noonday sun. I slid onto the leather seat beside him. Thomas and Antonio took the back seats. The scent of aged books and faint cigar smoke lingered in the air, a quiet testament to the decades of stories conjured within its cabin, and a stark contrast to The Tasty Burger we were heading to.

The car ride was quiet. James rolled the windows down and I breathed in the fresh air, trying to stay alert and awake. I was looking forward to the nap I had planned for after lunch. I'd asked Mary to keep Agatha until I returned. I don't think I could feed her another french fry for a long time.

Brandon was already seated at our favorite half-circle booth when we walked in. He waved us over with a plastic-covered menu.

After we ordered, Brandon wasted no time getting down to business.

"Owen has been released."

"What?" I tried to stand, but with Sleuths on either side, I only bruised my knees on the table.

Brandon fiddled with the plastic-covered menus in frustration. "Not only did his father hire some high-priced lawyer, but we had no evidence to hold him."

"So he could walk in here at any moment? Or the library?"

"You could get a restraining order," Thomas suggested.

"But he fed the puppy the french fry," Antonio argued as he patted me clumsily on the back.

"We don't know if the french fry was the culprit," James explained.

"Which is why I texted Randolph and asked him to review all of Emory's work. Including Janet and Ruthie's postmortems."

"That was you?" I said, and didn't hide the surprise in my voice.

"So you do respect The Sleuths," James said, as if he were stating a fact and not asking a question.

"I do. The truth is, you all intimidate me. All except…"

"Me," Antonio volunteered. "I know I am the one who is not the brightest blob."

I knew he meant to say bulb, but no one corrected him.

"No, Antonio. I was going to say Emory. He's young and, how do I say this… lacks social skills."

"Yes, he claimed to have solved the case a while ago at the library," Thomas said.

"So what do you need our help with?" James interjected, getting back to the case.

"I need you to not only be my eyes and ears, but I need to know some history about Ruthie, Janet, and anyone related to them."

"Simone had motive," Thomas offered. He quickly filled Brandon in on the conversation in the library earlier, and added his tainted two cents.

"That's good," he said as he jotted down some notes. "I'll go interview her later today."

Our food came and at the same time Owen swished through the door, looking more disheveled than usual. He made a beeline for our table.

"I didn't poison Agatha, Gabby, you've got to believe me."

I froze and clutched Antonio's arm. Antonio blurted out, "Miss Christie would never hurt a dog. I heard Gabby say that. She loved dogs."

Owen grabbed a chair from the table next to us and it squeaked in protest as he dragged it across the linoleum floor. "Exactly," Owen said as he straddled the chair. "I couldn't kill a dog. Agatha Christie wouldn't so neither would I."

I noted that he didn't say "I didn't murder anyone." So it was possible he still murdered Janet and Ruthie, and the rest of us sitting around the table were next.

"I think I'd like to go home now, James."

"Of course, dear." James signaled Tammy, our waitress, whose eyes grew wide when she caught sight of Owen.

"Gabby would like her food to go, please."

She grabbed my order and fumbled with it. It fell on the floor and she apologized. "Gabby, I'll get you a fresh order."

"Take mine," Brandon offered. "We have the same thing, right?"

"Of course." Her hands shook as she took Brandon's . He scooted out of the booth. I followed Tammy to the take-out counter.

"I thought Owen was in jail," she said.

"His dad got him some high-priced lawyer and he's out."

"Oh yeah," she said as she wrapped my burger in foil with The Tasty Burger Logo on it. "His family is loaded."

"I wonder why they didn't get him help."

She stuffed my burger and fries in a bag. "With his learning disability?"

"You know?"

"Owen and I dated when he first moved to town. I helped him with his college homework." She smoothed her apron and looked down at her shoes.

"Does anyone else know?"

"No, his father refused to acknowledge it. He chalks it up to laziness." She smiled a sad smile. "I thought he was the one, you know, but as soon as his father found out he was dating a college drop-out, he forbade him to see me."

"So he doesn't acknowledge you at all?"

"Pretty much. He wasn't always like that." She waved her hand in his direction. "When we were dating, he took care of himself and did well in his classes."

"With your help." I patted her hand in thanks as James joined us.

Tammy gave me a quiet nod before turning back to the kitchen, smoothing her apron like it could steady her.

James handed me the take-out bag. "Ready?"

Not really. But I nodded.

As we stepped outside, I caught one last glance at Owen through the diner window. He sat slouched over the table, hair unbrushed, shirt rumpled, eyes a little too bright. Off-kilter. But then again… hadn't he always been that way?

A chill snuck up my spine, settling between my shoulders.

I pulled my coat tighter around me.
Maybe it was just the wind.

CHAPTER 20
THE DATE

ONCE HOME, I pulled out my takeout bag. Agatha, whom I'd just set down, came running. It was a fight not to give Agatha a french fry. I finally had to crate her to keep her from licking one. I'm not sure why I thought a fry that didn't harm me in the least, except for possible long-term effects, would hurt her. Trauma does weird things to the brain. It convinces you that the worst possible thing that could happen, whether it was logical or not, would happen.

I fell asleep on the couch after finishing my Tasty Burger and fries. Agatha had curled up on my stomach and did the same.

I didn't know how long it had been when my phone buzzed, waking me up. I wiped a dribble of slobber off my cheek with my cardigan sleeve. The doorbell chimed and Agatha catapulted off my lap and barked as if the world was ending. I picked up my phone. A text from Randolph.

I read the text as I unwrapped my legs from the

overly ambitious cable-knit throw blanket and tumbled onto the floor. Agatha continued to yap at the door like someone had personally offended her.

While still tangled on the rug, losing the battle with the blanket and what little dignity I had left, I read Randolph's text.

> Emory and I are outside with your date.

My date? What time was it? I clicked out of the text message. It was 6:45 pm. How long had I slept? I freed my remaining entangled ankle from the throw blanket, placed a hand on the couch and pushed myself to my feet. It was at that exact same moment, I realized Agatha may be yapping for reasons other than an intruder.

Without checking my appearance, I grabbed the leash and said, "Hold it girl. I'll take you out."

I opened the door and waved the three men inside. "I've got to take her out before she does her business on the floor."

I ran with Agatha to the side yard, where the blue spruces separated my property from Miranda's, and prayed my hair wasn't sticking out in all directions.

"Hello, Gabby." I jumped as Miranda stepped out from between two spruces, holding a glass of wine and looking as perfectly polished as ever. "Three men knocking at your door."

"One is here for a date. The other two are coroners," I explained as I raked my finger through my hair and Agatha peed on a struggling daffodil.

"And I used to think you lived a boring life. Until last winter when a killer showed up at your house."

"Oh yeah. Thanks for being a great neighbor." I paused, then added, "...and friend."

"Of course we're friends. And in that line of thinking …" She glanced at me from top to bottom. "Friends help each other get ready for dates." She reached over and slipped the leash out my hand. "Be right back. Go into my house, grab a glass of wine, and wait for me."

Miranda tiptoed in her heels through the blue spruce trees and into my yard.

I obeyed – all except the wine. I didn't do well with alcohol of any kind. Two sips were like a bottle to my metabolism. A few sips of wine, and I either quoted Miss Marple and acted like an octogenarian, or professed my love for everyone within earshot.

I sat at the table, and after waiting five minutes, I poured myself a pinky finger's measure of the bottle sitting on the counter. One sip. That's it. Okay. Two. I've had a good lunch, it won't affect me much. Two minutes later, I'd drained the glass.

When Miranda returned, I set my wine glass down, confident it hadn't affected me in the least. She directed me to her bedroom. "I told that yummy detective to wait while you got ready and sent the coroners away. This is your date night after all."

"What did they want to tell me?"

"Something about wax or a ball of wax. I can't quite remember."

"Oh." That didn't make sense. I'd have to ask them later.

"This is perfect." She pulled a flowy silky jumper off a hanger. "Just your color too." It shimmered like the turquoise water in the commercials for fancy beach resorts.

"Go in the bathroom and wash your face with the cleanser on the sink. You look like Agatha after eating a treat."

"I fell asleep on the couch for —" She didn't let me finish before she patted me on the bottom and said, "Get going. You don't want the detective to get tired of waiting."

"Of course." With my face freshly scrubbed and oiled, she handed me the jumpsuit. "Go put this on and then we'll do your hair and makeup."

I obeyed and once seated at her makeup table, following up on the promise The Sleuths had made at The Tasty Burger, I asked, "What do you know about Simone and Ruthie?"

"Ruthie. I'm sorry she was murdered. I am. No one deserves that."

"But?" I stared at myself as she brushed my ginger hair into an updo, pulling my eyes so tight, they watered.

"That won't do," she said, releasing my hair. She plugged in a curling iron and brushed my hair out again. "Well, Ruthie and I crossed paths in the business world many times."

She twirled my hair around the curling iron and held it for a few seconds before releasing it. It bounced into a perfect spiral. "Let's just say she cut corners, slept with anyone and everyone to get to the top."

"Anyone and everyone? Can you clarify?"

She released another curl and smiled. "Why don't you ever wear your hair like this?"

"Because …"

"I know. You don't have time. Every beautiful woman should take the time to make the best of her looks."

Beautiful woman. Tucking that compliment away to bask in later.

"Is that what Ruthie did?"

Miranda released a curl and stepped back as if the iron had burned her. "Absolutely not. She didn't make the best of her looks. She used them. And used people and then discarded them like they were trash."

I was shocked at her anger. Maybe Ruthie had done something to her.

"Did she do anything to you?"

"No. I was only safe because I didn't have a husband to sleep with."

"Oh," I said, and left my mouth in an o shape while she finished the last curl.

"But she did sleep with a good friend of mine's husband. And it ruined her marriage and left her alone to take care of five children."

She applied a light lipstick.

"Shut your eyes." She gave my hair a liberal spray and then removed the towel she'd placed on my shoulders to protect my outfit. "There. Perfect."

As I stood and admired myself in the mirror, she added, "I don't know much about Simone's situation other than she lost her job. Thomas would know more about that. He was a town councilman then."

"Yes, I talked to him. He seems to think that Simone was more at fault than she lets on."

"If Ruthie was involved, then I'd question Ruthie's guilt before I would Simone's. But that's my opinion."

"Thank you for helping me get ready for my date."

Miranda leaned forward and gave me a quick hug. "Keep the outfit. It's not my color. Now go. Don't keep your date waiting."

She handed me a pair of gold heels. "Walk on the sidewalk. Don't go through the yard."

I walked out the front door and down the steps. Brandon was leaning against his dark blue 4Runner—reliable, low-maintenance, and exactly what I'd expect from someone who probably alphabetizes his sock drawer. It didn't purr or growl. It just showed up and got the job done. Kind of like him.

He smiled, waved, and said, "I put Agatha in her crate."

Oh good. I had been afraid Agatha would jump on me and ruin my outfit.

"You look amazing," he said as he opened my door.

"Better than the slobber-cheeked girl who answered the door half an hour ago?"

He chuckled. "Was that you?"

"No, that was my sloppy twin." I giggled.

Oh no, was the alcohol taking effect? I glanced at my phone. It had been how many hours since I'd eaten? Durn it. Did I drink a pinky of wine on an empty stomach? The sooner I got food in me the better.

"So where are we eating?" I asked, after he put the 4Runner in drive.

"There's a little Parisian restaurant half an hour from here. I thought we'd try that."

Half an hour. I couldn't do half an hour. Once the wine hit my bloodstream, I'd be professing my love for him or full-on quoting every Agatha Christie book I'd ever read.

"Is there somewhere closer?"

"You know as well as I do, The Tasty Burger is the only restaurant in Maplewood besides a few fast food ones near the interstate."

I flipped a curl up in the air and crossed my legs. "Yes, you're right. Drive on, my dear." And so it began. The I-love-you-super-sappy Gabby was on the loose and nothing would stop her. Except for a coffee and a full meal.

"My dear?" He swiveled his head and studied me. "You've been spending too much time with James."

"Mind if we grab a coffee first and I can tell you everything I learned from Miranda while she did my hair and makeup?"

Instead of pulling on the interstate, Brandon took the main street and pulled into the parking lot of The Daily Grind. "Do you want to get our coffee to go or drink it here?"

"Drink it here and then we can talk about the case before dinner." By that I meant, I'd pour a coffee down my throat and eat a few muffins to stave off the I-love-you-super-sappy Gabby.

"And then no talk about the case at dinner. That sounds romantic," he said, and smacked my knee with his large palm.

Not exactly a romantic gesture, but I knew — the I-love-you-super-sappy Gabby gobbled stuff like that up. Once, at the library Christmas staff party, I'd taken a sip of wine and told the fifty year-old very married janitor that I loved him. He had returned the phrase and brushed it off, as Brittany, my honorary guest, had made me go in the bathroom and splash cold water on my face. Thankfully, the I-love-you-super-sappy Gabby had been short-lived that evening. To help me save face, Brittany had made sure I told the whole staff that I loved them while handing out their gifts.

We took a corner booth in The Daily Grind and ordered lattes. I asked for extra heavy cream. Anything to stave off professions of love, or any other embarrassing thing I might say.

"And I'll have two banana nut muffins."

Brandon looked surprised, but didn't say "but we're going to eat dinner."

He grasped both my hands while we waited for our order. "I'm so glad you agreed to go to dinner with me. And I'll say it again, Gabby. You look amazing."

No you can't say it again. Don't say stuff like that. But it was too late. He'd said it.And the wine was doing its work.

"I'm so glad too. Let's get married."

Brandon's gray eyes widened. A mixture of shock and deep, soul-crushing amusement flickered across his ridiculously handsome face.

"I would marry you right now if we had a minister and a cake."

The words just *fell* out of my mouth. Like, no warning, no internal debate, just full send. The wine had obliterated my common sense and replaced it with a Hallmark script.

Brandon blinked. "What?"

Oh no. *Oh no no no.*

But the I-love-you-super-sappy Gabby was in full control now, steamrolling over logic like a runaway train. I pressed forward, gripping his hands like we were about to recite our vows. "I mean, why wait? Love is fleeting. Life is short. You think you have time to be normal and take things slow, but one day you wake up and you're eighty and you've wasted decades *not* being married to the love of your life—"

"Gabby."

I squeezed his hands tighter. "We could elope! I've always thought a courthouse wedding would be so romantic. Just you, me, and a judge who probably hates love but does it anyway because it pays the bills."

Brandon was staring at me, his lips twitching like he was torn between running for his life and pulling out a ring.

"I'd take your last name," I barreled on, *because apparently, I wasn't finished ruining my dignity.* "Gabby Hale. Ooooh, that sounds sophisticated. Or we could hyphenate! Gabby Keats-Hale. Very strong. Or—*oh my gosh*—we could combine them! Kale! Haler? Kaler!"

Brandon coughed, definitely choking back laughter. "Wow. That's… a lot of commitment for a coffee date."

I gasped. "You're right. We don't even have rings. I could use my muffin wrapper."

And that was it. Brandon *lost it.* Full, deep, chest-rumbling laughter. People turned. The barista smirked.

And that's when reality *slammed* into me.

Oh. *Oh no.*

The I-love-you-super-sappy Gabby had *struck again.*

A figure rose from the booth behind us and jerked me up by one arm. "Let's go, Gabby."

"Brittany, what are you doing on my date?" I stumbled after her and she sat me down in the booth she'd just vacated.

"Verity, can you get Gabby's coffee over here right away? And whatever else she ordered."

Verity gave us a quick wave and rushed behind the counter. I waved and shouted, "I'm getting married, Verity!"

"Oh no you're not," Brittany said as she shoved my hand down. "She's not getting married," she called out, as if daring anyone in a ten-mile radius to challenge her.

A few customers chuckled.

"Did you give her alcohol?" Brittany challenged Brandon.

Brandon fumbled. "No … I… Miranda helped her get ready."

Verity set my coffee down and Brittany warned her, "Not a word to anyone, got it?"

"Don't worry. Remember, she told my dad she loved him at the Maplewood Library Christmas Staff party. He still thinks it is a hoot."

"Now you know what the rumor mill is like around here…"

Verity held an imaginary key to her lips and turned it. "I can't say the same for the customers or the detective."

I slurped my coffee loudly. Brittany had moved to Brandon's booth. "I think you should go," she said. "I'll get her home."

"I didn't give her anything to drink, I promise."

I leaned over the booth back and pawed at Brittany. "Hey, are you stealing my groom?"

"Drink your coffee, Gabby."

"I'll be going then." Brandon stood and exited quickly.

I don't remember Brittany driving me home. I woke up tucked in bed in my favorite plaid flannel PJs with Brittany snoring beside me.

At least it wasn't Brandon. That was something. But why couldn't I remember anything from my date— except going to The Daily Grind? My thoughts felt like a scratched record, skipping over something important.

Then it hit me. A wave of panic crashed over me, stealing my breath.

I grabbed Brittany's arm and shook her. Hard. "How did my date go?" My voice came out half demand, half prayer.

She groaned, rolling away from me. "You proposed," she mumbled into her pillow. Then, with an irritated huff she grumbled, "Now leave me alone and let me sleep."

My stomach dropped. Proposed? As in marriage?

I scrambled for my phone, my heart pounding like a war drum. "Proposed to *whom*?"

Brittany sighed dramatically, flipping onto her back and cracking one eye open. "Brandon," she muttered, before yanking the blanket over her head.

The room spun. My knees gave out, and I collapsed onto the bed like a marionette with its strings cut.

Well. That was it. I could never leave the house again.

CHAPTER 21
THE CONFRONTATION

I DIDN'T LEAVE the house on Sunday. I couldn't. After proposing to Brandon—yes, *proposing*—thanks to two and a half sips of wine, the only thing I had the nerve to face was my favorite mug of coffee and the quiet judgment of my ceiling fan. Brittany had rescued me, made sure I got home, and then—in true Brittany fashion—promptly told The Sleuths. All of them.

I didn't text Brandon. He didn't text me. The silence felt like mercy… and mortification.

Monday morning I met The Sleuths in the fishbowl room.

Antonio led with, "When is the wedding, Gabby?"

Emory looked disappointed. Did he have a crush on me?

"Don't worry, I'm not getting married. That was just the wine talking," I explained.

Emory gave me a quick smile. Antonio smacked his doughy hands on his thighs. "No wedding?"

That was the moment I caved. I told them everything—from the wine and the cafe to offering to make a ring made out of a muffin wrapper, and the shocked look on Brandon's face. Every cringey detail.

James offered a soft gasp, then another *"My dear."* And then another. By the fifth one, I was crying.

"I've ruined it."

"Of course you haven't," Thomas replied. "I can write you an apology speech if you like."

Randolph shared, "Ah, the hippocampus—the little librarian of your brain—doesn't do well with alcohol. Too much wine, and it stops filing memories properly. That's why you blacked out, kid. Your brain hit the delete button while your mouth kept running."

"Can we not talk about this anymore? Today's meeting of The Sleuths is supposed to be about all the facts you've gathered for..." I hesitated. I didn't want to say Detective Brandon, so instead I said, "The police."

James patted me on the back. "Yes, let's get to work, my dear."

"Is Brittany coming?" Thomas asked.

"No, she has an interview with The Grandview." I pulled my phone out. "She did ask me to record the meeting today though."

Allison hovered in the fishbowl room door. "Am I late?"

"No, we're just getting started." I turned to The Sleuths. "I invited Allison. I hope you don't mind."

"Moms are good at overhearing gossip." She took the coffee I handed her. "It's kind of our superpower."

"How so?" Emory asked.

"Well, when we go to the grocery store or out for coffee, people just ignore us. We're the stay-at-home-moms. They assume we lost our ability to hear, and our brains, when we decided to leave the workforce."

"Oh," Emory said. "I'm sorry for that."

"We can't get the board out. Too many patrons. Allison, can you use your notes app and record?"

We gathered around the table and started listing everything we knew—at least, what hadn't already been twisted by speculation or town gossip.

She pulled her phone out of her bag and clicked on an app. "Sure, *Mrs. Hale.*"

"I'm never going to live that down, am I?"

"Nope," she said. "Okay, I'm ready."

Owen was still out on bail.

Simone had motive to kill Ruthie, but not Janet.

Janet's son had tried to sell the copy of *A Murder is Announced* at a local antique store – The Dusty Page.

I shared what Miranda had told me about Ruthie's habit of sleeping her way to the top. "She slept with one of Miranda's friends' husbands and ruined her marriage, leaving her with five children to raise alone."

Allison paused typing and asked, "Did she say who the friend was?"

"No."

"How many families in Maplewood have five children?" Randolph asked. "Maybe we do some research?"

"That's a good idea, but I have a better one." I pulled out my phone and shot a quick text to Miranda.

> What's the name of your friend? The one who Ruthie ruined her marriage and left her to raise five kids.

I knew it was long as far as texts go, but Miranda had said Ruthie had slept with many of the men of Maplewood. I wanted to be clear about who I was asking about.

"Just remember if we don't catch the Agatha Christie copycat killer, he could strike again," James warned. Just like they did in the Christie novels.

"It's been almost a week since Ruthie was murdered…" I stopped. "Wait, Randolph, Emory, what else did you find in the review of Agatha's stomach contents?"

Randolph looked puzzled. "We told Miranda. I emphatically said, 'tell Gabby we found traces of wax in Agatha's stomach.'"

"She couldn't remember what you said."

"We should have waited and talked to you," Emory lamented.

"She wouldn't remember either." Antonio pantomimed drinking from a wine glass. "Because she was sauced. Get it? I make pizza." He chuckled at his own joke.

No, I was never going to live my drunk proposal down. The I-love-you-super-sappy Gabby would be the talk of the town.

James smacked his thighs. "Agatha licked Cora's shoes."

"And she makes candles," I offered. I stood and held the one she'd given us that night, feeling guilty we hadn't used it as we promised.

"So that solves the mystery of the candle wax," Randolph said.

Nobody had heard any more information that we didn't already know. We wrapped up the meeting.

"See you later at book club?" I asked everyone.

"I wouldn't miss it for the world," James said. Everyone else promised to come. I wished I could stay home. I hadn't seen everyone since being arrested and proposing marriage to the very person who arrested me.

———

That evening, I pulled the letter board out and again questioned leaving the book title – *A Murder Is Announced* – spelled out. As I once again debated changing it, a book club member entered.

"Hello! Anyone here?"

"Oh, Cora. Welcome!"

"I brought you another candle." As she approached me, she reached in her leather satchel and pulled out another kaleidoscope candle.

"Thank you, you didn't have to."

She peered around me, trying to get a glimpse into the fishbowl room. "Did you like the one I gave you for The Sleuths?"

"With everything going on, I forgot about it. I'm sorry."

"Oh yes, of course. I'm sorry about Agatha."

"You'll get a kick of out of this. The coroner found wax in Agatha's stomach."

"Wax?" She blanched white. "Oh yes, it drips on my shoes when I'm making candles." She placed her hand over her mouth and let out a nervous laugh. "That's funny."

"Yes, the vet says Agatha needs to eat more dog food, and less of, well everything else."

At the mention of her name, Agatha joined us and sniffed Cora's shoes and growled.

"That's right, girl. No more wax for you," Cora said as she backed up.

"Is there book club tonight or not?"

Owen.

"Owen, I'm not sure you should be here," I said.

"I promise you, Gabby, I didn't poison your dog," He repeated.

Before I could say another word, a group of book club members descended on me. I retreated to the fishbowl room and set out the muffins. I couldn't exactly tell Owen he had to leave—he was free. The police couldn't pin the poisoning on him because, as the vet and Randolph explained, Agatha's stomach was full of pretty much everything.With a cup of coffee in hand, I exited the fishbowl room. The book club members were all talking at the same time, like angry buzzing bees.

"Everyone grab a cup of coffee and a muffin. We'll start in five minutes."

"I'm not staying here as long as he is here." Cora pointed at Owen. "One of us is next, aren't we?"

"All so you can write your bestseller," Simone added in her best school marm voice, peering down her glasses at him.

"Listen everyone, Owen has a right to be here. The police haven't officially charged him with anything." I couldn't believe I was standing up for the man who'd poisoned my dog.

Agatha had taken up residence as his feet. He reached down and patted her. Then quickly held his hands in the air. "I'm not feeding her anything. And again, I did not poison her or murder anyone."

Thomas stood and cleared his throat. "Friends, Gabby is right. Owen has the right to be here. We are here to talk about our latest read, *A Murder Is Announced*."

James stood and continued, "So let's do that. Grab a coffee and a muffin and then take your seats."

The front door opened just wide enough for Allison to squeeze in first, juggling a covered plate and her usual mix of calm and chaos.

"I brought lemon bars," she said, offering them like a peace offering and a conversation starter all in one. "And yes, Ned knows I'm here. He made me pinky promise not to get murdered."

I laughed. "Tell him we'll do our best."

She stepped further inside, shoulders easing once she saw a few familiar faces and felt no immediate tension in the air. Behind her came Miranda, a vision of effortless polish in tailored black slacks and a soft blue silk blouse, heels clicking softly on the wood floor.

"Gabby." She greeted me with a warm smile and a light touch on my arm, the kind of gesture that said "I see you, even if we're both pretending this is just another book club meeting."

"I almost didn't come," she admitted under her breath. Then with a wry smile, added, "But curiosity won."

I glanced over her shoulder at Cora, already seated and flipping through the book like she hadn't read it twice already. Miranda caught my glance and followed it. She waved at Cora before sitting next to her.

Allison hovered near the snack table, scanning the room. I motioned for her to grab a seat beside Miranda. Two women who didn't know each other, brought together by murder mysteries.

The room was filling, and the low hum of conversation swirled around us—wary, yes, but laced with anticipation. The kind of energy that builds right before the plot twist.

I was going to have to pull a newer copy of *A Murder Is Announced* from the shelves since our original copy, the one donated by Janet, had been stolen. I set my coffee down on the cafe table I used during book club, and there it was. The original copy sans the cover. I did a 180 glance around the book club.

Brett gave me a wave. "I'm sorry," he mouthed. I left my spot at the front of the group and went to greet him, while the rest of the book club loaded up cups and plates.

"I'm so sorry," he said.

"Are you staying?" I asked.

"My mom loved this book club. I thought I owed it to her to join." He ran a trembling hand through his hair. "Is that okay?"

"Are you okay?" I asked back.

He sniffed and pulled out a tissue and wiped his nose. "It's just hitting me, you know. I had coffee with my mom every morning. Just to talk, you know. I find myself driving to her house every morning on autopilot."

"Does it bother you that Owen is here?"

"Owen didn't murder anyone, especially not my mother."

"How do you know that?"

"He's just a mixed up kid. I'm breaking some rules here, but you should know. I did the psych eval on him a few years back."

"So you know about his dyslexia?"

"Yes. And his father, who stormed into the office and dragged poor Owen out as if he were a criminal, not a brilliant kid with a learning challenge."

"You said, especially not your mother. How could you know that?"

"When I saw Owen around town and how much he's deteriorated, I asked Mom to tutor him, off the books of course, so his father wouldn't find out."

"Gabby, shall we get started, my dear?" James said from my cafe table.

"One sec," I replied, and then turned back to Brett. "And she agreed?"

"She started the week before she died."

I stepped away to start the meeting, but he pulled me back and added. "And according to her, was making great progress. He loved working with her."

I walked in jerky marionette fashion back to my cafe table. Owen had no motive to kill the person who could potentially help him finally write his bestseller. Or a motive to kill Ruthie.

Didn't Miranda say you had to have a husband to sleep with?

That narrowed the list. Ruthie's trail of destruction wasn't random—it was targeted. And only the women whose marriages she wrecked, or whose lives she set on fire with a single affair, would've had real motive.

That meant Owen—awkward, slightly unhinged Owen—was probably innocent. And the killer?

The killer was likely sitting here, at book club. Watching. Listening. Planning the next Agatha Christie copycat murder while passing around lemon bars and pretending to care about this month's read.

CHAPTER 22

THE END

"I DON'T KNOW how I made it through book club," I said to James as I leaned heavily on a chair.

"That argument about who the killer was in *A Murder Is Announced*, really?" He straightened his collar. "We know who finished the book."

He glanced around at the guilty members who argued it couldn't be Letty. "I mean she wasn't even Letty. She was her sister."

"That gives me an idea," I said as I waved goodbye at Simone and Thomas, who left debating her dismissal from the school *again*.

"Is there a romance budding there, do you think?" James asked.

I hung my head in my hands. "I'm the wrong person to ask about romance. I ruined my chance with Brandon."

"May I ask you a personal question?"

I looked up and outright laughed. "A personal question? The whole town knows every personal detail of my life."

He chuckled and then continued, "Did he say no?"

"Did who say no to what?" My mind was busy sorting thoughts on the copycat killer and my relationship with Brandon like they were laundry.

"Did Brandon say no to your marriage proposal?"

"No, he looked shocked at first, and then he laughed."

James grabbed his hat and plopped it on his head. "So he didn't say no."

I frowned. "But that doesn't mean I didn't ruin it."

He gave me a gentle look, the kind that made it hard to argue. "If he laughed, Gabby, that means he's still with you in it. Maybe not ready for rings and vows, but still there."

He didn't leave right away. Just stood there a moment, smoothing the brim of his hat like he was waiting for me to catch up to what he already knew.

He gave me a quick peck on the cheek. "See you tomorrow, my dear."

"If I'm not the next Agatha Christie copycat killer victim, that is," I joked.

"If the discussion during this evening's meeting is any indication of the group's knowledge on Agatha Christie, then no one here is the copycat killer."

A few people lingered, including Owen, who I guessed wanted to apologize again. And state his innocence.

"Gabby, can I show you something?" Right on cue. "Janet was helping me with this." He shoved his journal under my nose. Instead of only words, he'd drawn pictures and symbols. "It's pictograms. See, I have a key." He flipped to the back of the journal and pulled the key out of a zipper pocket that I had missed.

"That's why you were so upset about losing your journal," I stated matter-of-factly.

"Yes, it was like I finally had a way to communicate in writing and I lost it. With Janet dead, I didn't know who to turn to."

"And you couldn't ask your father for help," I filled in.

"Yes."

"Well, there is a certain young waitress at The Tasty Burger who I know for a fact would be happy to help you."

He grinned and his blue eyes twinkled. "You think so?"

"I know so." I patted him on the shoulder. "But before you go see her, you might want to..." I didn't know how to put it delicately, so I waved my hand over his filthy tattered army surplus jacket.

"Got it. Clean myself up and don't drink any wine. I'm sorry, I couldn't resist." He smacked me on the back with his journal.

"Haha. Owen, I think you and I are going to be friends, aren't we?"

He nodded and shoved his journal in his briefcase, snapping it shut. Then he gave me a salute and left.

A few other patrons trickled out behind him, coats zipped and books tucked under their arms, offering polite waves and quiet goodnights as they went. The library settled into silence.

I hummed as I cleaned up the coffee and snack area

in the fishbowl room. I paused and lit the candle Cora had left the other day.

That left Cora and me.

Brittany texted me:

> Murder Mystery Movie Night tonight

She hadn't been able to attend for the second time in a row. This time because of the job interview she'd had this afternoon. They had requested she write an article as some sort of a test. An article that had nothing to do with a copycat killer. Something she dreaded writing about — climate change. It was the climate change article that got her intern sacked. The editor of The Grandview asked her to rework the intern's article and submit it.

I replied to her text with:

> Yes. Don't forget to include The weather isn't just weird—it's downright moody.

She texted back:

> Funny. See you in half an hour

I'd better get a move on if I was going to make it home in half an hour. As I cleaned and hummed, my mind replayed all the conversations of the day — the clues, the discussion, the last thing James said before he left.

"There is no Agatha Christie copycat killer."

"What did you say?"

I turned from the coffee maker and stuck a hand on my heart. "Oh, Cora, you scared me. I thought everyone had left."

"I thought you could use some help," she said. "Everyone always leaves a mess for you to clean up. I know how it feels. My kids do that."

I handed her the container of cleaning wipes. "Thank you. How many kids do you have?"

She scrubbed the surface where the muffins had sat. "I wouldn't call them kids anymore. Three teens and two in their early twenties. Off at college now."

"Five kids," I said.

She stopped scrubbing. "What was that?"

"Don't mind me. I'm just talking to myself."

"You said there was no copycat killer."

"Yes, I did. I'm just reviewing everything I've learned the past few days, and it just doesn't add up. I can't put my finger on it."

"Oh, I see you lit the candle I left for you and The Sleuths the other day."

Cora smiled—tight, too bright—and set the cleaning wipe down with more care than it needed. Then she backed away from me, slowly, one hand hovering near her nose.

"This room makes every smell more potent," she said lightly.

For half a second, I thought the citrusy cleaning wipes were to blame—strong, maybe, but nothing worth retreating over. Then I caught the flicker in her eyes. Not on me. On the candle.

The soft, steady flame danced in its delicate glass jar,

filling the fishbowl room with something floral and faintly sweet. Sage, maybe. Vanilla. Nothing offensive. Nothing alarming.

But her hand was already on the door handle.

My stomach dipped.

Miss Marple always said people revealed themselves in the small things. A twitch of the eye, a misplaced compliment, a smile that stretched too far. They didn't have to confess—they just had to *react*.

And Cora was reacting.

"You okay?" I asked, my voice calm even as the hairs on my arms stood up. "You look a little... flushed."

"Just sensitive to strong scents," she said, her hand tightening around the doorknob.

Funny. She'd gifted that candle to The Sleuths. Wrapped it herself. And now she couldn't stand to be in the same room with it?

My eyes shifted to the flickering wick, to the faint shimmer on the inside of the glass, and then—just for a moment—to the vent above the door. This room *did* trap smells. And chemicals. And intentions.

"I think," I said slowly, "that I've had quite enough ambiance for one day."

Her eyes met mine. Calculating. Cool. And just a little too late.

I dove for the door, but she slammed something hard against the side of my head. Stars sparked across my vision as I stumbled. I managed to shove Agatha out just as the door closed—but the latch didn't catch cleanly.

The lock clicked. Then wavered. A metallic *clunk*.

She jiggled the handle.

It was jammed.

We were locked in—but not how she planned.

"Blow out the candle," she screamed.

"It was you."

"Yes, it was me. Oh, how long ago did you light the candle?"

I tried to remember. It was when I started cleaning. I clutched my chest, my heart was beating too fast. I gasped for air.

"We're dying," she said, putting the lid on the candle.

I rolled over on my back and gingerly touched the back of my head. I was bleeding.

The world swam in and out of focus. My head throbbed where Cora had hit me, and the cold floor pressed against my cheek.

Agatha lunged at the glass, barking—mouth wide, teeth bared, nails skittering wildly against the doorframe. Her fur bristled, and she kept glancing back, like she was ready to bolt for help if someone would just listen.

My stomach twisted. The scent was thick, cloying. My chest felt heavy, like my ribs were wrapped in iron bands.

I forced myself up, my limbs trembling. Cora stood near the door, her hand still gripping whatever she'd used to knock me down—a thick hardcover, *Murder at the Vicarage*.

She'd hit me with a cozy mystery. The irony almost made me laugh.

But then I saw her face. Pale. Sweaty.

Panic.

Then it hit me.

Agatha.

The vet.

I swallowed against the rising nausea. "The candle," I gasped. "That's why she got sick."

Cora nodded, her lips twitching at the corners. "Laced with arsenic."

I recoiled, my pulse hammering. "Oh my—" My stomach clenched. "Oh my gosh."

My breath caught as the pieces slid into place. "That's how you killed Janet—inside her locked room."

Cora let out a breathy laugh, shaking her head. "It was supposed to be for Ruthie."

I barely heard her. The blood roared in my ears, my body cold and clammy all at once.

"I—I didn't know," I stammered. "I mixed them up. I thought it was just scented wax."

Cora's gaze snapped to mine, sharp and furious. "You fool."

I flinched.

She took a step forward, swaying slightly. "Do you know what Ruthie did to me? She stole my husband. Disgraced him. He divorced me and left me with five kids while he chased younger women."

She was spiraling now, her breath ragged, her hands curling into fists.

"And then," she spat, "she ran for town council. Pretended to be this perfect, moral woman. And the worst part?" Her eyes glistened. "She came to book club. *My* book club."

A bitter laugh escaped her lips.

"So I thought... why not let her go out doing something she loved? A candle for her office, a warm glow, the sweet scent of vanilla… I didn't mean to kill…"

I sucked in a sharp breath.

"You didn't mean to kill Janet," I whispered.

Cora's face twisted. "She got the wrong candle and that's on you."

I leaned back on the glass wall of the fishbowl room. "But the whole copycat killer story?"

"Your friend Brittany started that. I was happy to let it run its course." She sat down heavily and grunted. "And Owen, the perfect scapegoat."

A loud bang rattled the glass walls of the fishbowl room.

My heart leaped. Agatha barked louder, more frantic. Someone was out there.

I struggled to sit up, my vision swimming. The air felt heavier, my body sluggish.

Another bang.

The sound of shattering glass.

Cora screamed as the door was thrown open.

Fresh air rushed in, cold and sharp.

I gasped, sucking in oxygen, my lungs burning. A shadow loomed in the doorway.

Then everything went black.

CHAPTER 23
THE EXPLANATION

I WOKE and rubbed the sleep from my eyes.

Brittany sat in an olive green faux leather recliner, the kind you find in hospital rooms.

"Where am I?" I croaked.

"You're awake. Take it easy, Gabby." She didn't answer my question—just straightened my sheets, tucked me back in, and hit the call button.

"It was Cora." I struggled with the covers, again.

"Yes, it was."

"Is she…?"

"Dead? No. She's been kicking and screaming for the last hour."

"Oh," I said. "Did you get the job?"

"I did but that's a conversation for later."

Nurse Bella entered and grabbed my wrist. "The patient is awake."

"When can the patient go home?" I asked. Bella was no stranger to me. We'd gone to high school together, and let's just say she wasn't one of the nice girls. When we graduated and she applied for nursing school after a few years of pre-med, she made it abundantly clear that I'd chosen the lesser career.

So while she should have been acknowledging both Brittany and I as former classmates, she instead did her job succinctly, apparently leaving her bedside manner at the nurse's station.

She grabbed my chart at the end of the bed and scribbled something. "The doctor will be in shortly, patient."

Brittany stood and towered over her. "The patient asked a question."

"Brandon asked me to call him when she woke. That's your answer." She swished out of the room as if she was wearing an evening gown and heels instead of lilac-colored scrubs.

"I wish she was the copycat killer. I have plenty to write about her. Did you hear how she said *Brandon?*"

"Maybe after the way I acted the other night, Brandon is dating other people."

She sat down heavily in her chair and grunted. "If that's true, I can write a thing or two about him."

"Can I have some water?"

"Nurse Bella should have asked you what you needed." She stood and poured a glass of water from the yellow plastic hospital pitcher and handed it to me.

"Is Agatha okay?" I asked, my brain finally clearing, just enough for me to scold myself for missing what had been right in front of me all along. It's never the clues we don't see—it's the ones we look at and convince ourselves mean something else.

"Yes, Miranda has her."

"Oh, good. Thank you." I downed the glass of water. "There is no Agatha Christie copycat killer," I said when I finished.

"What?" She pulled out her phone. "Permission to record?"

"Of course. I'll tell you everything."

While we waited for Brandon to come interview me, I told Brittany everything. I started from James' offhanded statement about the murder mystery illiterates in book club and how there couldn't be a copycat killer.

"What else?"

"There were little things that weren't adding up." I cleared my throat. "I could really use a good coffee."

"I doubt they have those here, but I could call someone."

I glanced at the clock. "Emory," I stated. I didn't want to wake James or any of the other Sleuths. "I want to confirm something with him anyway."

"I'll shoot him a text."

"Like I was saying, little things. For instance, in Owen's favorite Agatha Christie novel, which he's checked out ten times in the audio version…might be his favorite because it is one of the few we have on audio…" *I'll have to fix that*, I said to myself.

"I don't get it."

"I'll explain later. But in *And Then There Were None*, each of the ten people had committed a crime and the killer was serving justice."

"So knocking off random book club members is definitely off-book."

"Especially since Janet was helping Owen by

tutoring him and giving him some tools to help with his dyslexia."

"Oh…"

"You can't print that part. It's his story, not mine."

"Got it. Go on."

We'd only been talking for ten minutes when Emory showed up. "One double shot Americano."

"How'd you get here so fast?"

"Oh, I'm not supposed to say."

Brittany cleared her throat.

"Please Emory."

"I was downstairs with the rest of The Sleuths waiting to make sure you were okay."

I peered behind him as if they would appear out of thin air. "And they're still down there?"

"Not exactly…"

"You can't go in there. The patient is resting until Brandon gets here."

"Balderdash." James's voice echoed through the hallway.

"The patient's name is Gabby. But you know that, Bella. You always were too big for your britches."

I straightened instinctively at the sound of her voice. Simone was in full-on teacher mode, and apparently, my brain still knew how to report for duty. She could probably wake the dead with that tone—which, around here, was starting to feel less like a joke and more like a job description.

"And that's *Detective* Brandon to you," Antonio corrected. "He is marrying Gabby."

"Well, I…" Bella's voice trailed off as she stomped down the hall away from my room.

Sixty seconds later, I was sipping the double shot Americano and eating a chocolate chip walnut muffin surrounded by friends.

"I'm glad you are all here," I said as I wiped a tear from my cheek. "I thought I was going to die in the fishbowl room."

"I'm afraid the fishbowl room is broken." Antonio patted my leg.

"I wasn't there to see it, but according to Greg, Brandon grabbed the axe from the back of the library and freed you from the fishbowl room."

"He broke the glass?" Brittany asked, typing furiously. "This story is getting better by the second."

With the help of The Sleuths, I explained why Cora was the culprit.

"It was the candles," Emory said. "They had arsenic in them."

Randolph added, "Yes. I suspected something was off when Emory found wax in Agatha's stomach."

"She licks everyone's shoes." Antonio chuckled.

"So right you are, Antonio. The poor dear licked the arsenic wax off Cora's shoes."

I pulled the sheets up to my neck and shuddered. "When a bunch of candles 'accidentally' fell out of her bag at the library, Cora let me keep a sage one. Then she 'welcomed' me to take a lavender candle home and burn it right away—that was the night Owen was arrested." I paused, thinking back. Had the whole *oops-the-candles-fell-out* act been a setup to slip me one?

"She wanted to kill you," Simone said. "She knew you were smart and would figure it out."

"She said the sage candle was for The Sleuths,"

James added, his brow furrowed. "Remember, Gabby? She told you to light it during our next meeting."

A chill crept over me.

If I'd burned the candle she gave me that night... I'd already be dead.

And if The Sleuths had lit theirs at the meeting—they'd be gone too.

Neat. Efficient. Exactly how Cora planned it.

"That's right, she did."

"I don't think she meant to kill us," Thomas added. "Surely not."

"If we would have shut the door and lit the candle..." Randolph ran his finger across his throat. "I'll bet, knowing Cora made that candle to kill you, and the wax she got on her shoes from it almost killed Agatha, it had more arsenic than the others."

"She didn't mean to kill Janet. She and Ruthie both left their candles at book club last week. I ran out after them to hand them back—but they looked the same, so I just gave one to each of them."

"You got them mixed up."

"Yes, so it's my fault Janet is dead."

"Nonsense, my dear. Cora is the guilty one. Not you." James's words soothed me, but didn't erase the guilt I felt.

The door swung open hard enough to rattle the glass.

Brandon stepped in, eyes scanning the room like he expected a crime scene. "What's going on here? This is police business," he snapped, his glare locking onto Antonio like he'd just trampled sacred ground.

Antonio raised both hands and grinned. "Settle

down, fiancé! Come on, everyone, let's leave him to say hello to his betrothed." He chuckled all the way to the door, waving the others out like he was parting the sea.

Brandon's face turned fire alarm red.

I didn't even try to hide the smirk tugging at the corner of my mouth. Antonio had a gift for dramatic exits, and Brandon had a gift for looking guilty about feelings he hadn't admitted yet.

"Pretty sure being mistaken for my fiancé isn't a felony," I murmured, mostly to myself—though Brandon's ears turned an even deeper shade of red.

He looked like he might argue, but thankfully, The Sleuths were already halfway out the door, snickering like middle schoolers at a school dance.

"Sure, you keep telling yourself that," Brittany said as she grabbed her backpack. "Come on everyone, you heard Antonio."

As soon as The Sleuths exited, Bella waltzed in. "Brandon you're here. Let me know if you need anything." Her cheeks were glowing and she tucked a strand of hair behind an ear, her tell-tale flirty move from high school. I guess some things never changed.

Brandon kept his eyes on me. "That will be all, nurse."

Yes! Yes! Yes! He wasn't into her. He hadn't been fooled by her flirty charms.

She stood frozen in the doorway, confused as to why her charms hadn't worked, I'm sure.

Brandon turned to face her. "Shouldn't you be asking if the patient, Gabby, needs anything?"

She turned and scuttled out the door like a squirrel being chased by a dog.

"I thought you were dead," he said as he grasped both my hands.

I wasn't sure what to say. I hadn't had any wine, but I still didn't trust myself in his presence. What if I proposed again? So I swallowed and said, "I thought I was dead too."

"I'm going to have to ask you a few questions. Then I'll let you rest."

"I heard you took an axe to the fishbowl room."

"I did. I'm sorry. It's going to need some hefty repairs."

"Thank you for saving me."

He cleared his throat and sat back in a chair. "So… Cora is squawking like a parrot. She's pretty much told us everything, but I need your side of the story."

The arsenic was either having its second wind, or the adrenaline had worn off. I didn't want to share everything again.

"She locked me in the fishbowl room with the arsenic candle."

My eyes fluttered, heavy as anvils. No matter how hard I fought it, consciousness slipped through my fingers like sand. I forced one eye open. He was still there, notepad in hand, watching me with that unreadable expression.

I needed to stay awake. I needed to answer his questions. But exhaustion wrapped around me, warm and inescapable, pulling me under.

Candles flickered. Soft music played. A bouquet of white roses filled my hands.

I turned—and there was Brandon, looking devastatingly handsome in a tux, grinning like he'd just won the lottery.

Oh no.

I tried to stop myself, but it was too late.

I beamed up at him. "I do," I sighed dreamily.

Somewhere, far away, a chair scraped against tile.

"Gabby?" His voice was closer now, laced with something that sounded like amusement—and maybe a little concern. "Are you okay?"

I forced my eyes open just in time to see Detective Brandon leaning over me, brows furrowed—but there was the faintest flicker of amusement in his eyes, like he wasn't sure whether to scold me or laugh.

Then he turned toward the door. "She's mumbling about marrying me—can someone get the nurse?"

If I could have disappeared into the hospital bed, I would have.

CHAPTER 24
A FRESH START

I'D BEEN HOME for two days when Brandon stopped by.

"Is this an official visit?" Brittany asked when she answered the door. "I thought the case was wrapped up," she added.

"A few more loose ends. But this is unofficial." He stepped past her and stood in the living room. I sat on the couch with Agatha on my lap. Well, she was on my lap until she saw him. She jumped down and wagged her tail as she licked his shoes.

"You solved it, you know, Agatha," he complimented as he patted her head.

"I thought you said this wasn't an official visit," Brittany replied.

"I brought Agatha some doggie treats," he said to me, and handed me a paper bag with a Friendly Pet sticker on it.

"I guess you're ignoring me," Brittany said over her

shoulder as she stepped into the kitchen. "Don't mind me, I'll make some coffee."

Brandon stood in the middle of the living room looking as if he didn't know what to do with himself. He clasped his hands in front of him. He wasn't wearing his detective clothing. His face showed that oh-so-handsome day-old stubble, and his eyes glowed silver-gray like the sky did after a spring storm. His jeans looked comfy and well worn.

"Have a seat," I offered, and patted the cushion next to me on the couch.

He complied, and Agatha hopped on his lap. He patted her, which gave his hands something to do.

"Thank her already," Brittany shouted from the kitchen.

"I already did and I brought her treats," Brandon said as he fluffed Agatha's fur. If she were a cat, she'd be purring.

"I think she meant me."

"Oh, thank you for not dying."

"And solving the case," Brittany said as she joined us, carrying a tray laden with freshly baked white chocolate cranberry cookies and coffees.

"Thank you," he said.

She handed him a mug of coffee. "There. That wasn't so hard."

"Didn't you get some big city job? Aren't you moving away or something?"

"Yes, I did get a job at The Grandview Herald. I'm not moving. It's a weekly column and I can submit my work online, from right here in Maplewood." She reached over and tucked a blanket around my legs as if I were a sick child.

"Oh, congratulations." He took a sip of coffee. "Could we have a bit of privacy?"

"No. You cannot. I'm nursing Gabby back to health and I'm not leaving her for a second until she is back to one hundred percent."

"You left me for fifteen minutes to talk to Miranda next door earlier," I commented as I pulled at the blanket and freed my legs.

She winked. "That was to tell her not to give you anymore wine. We all know how that turned out last time."

"Okay, why don't you go talk to Miranda, again?"

"Tell you what, I'll go walk Agatha. Will that give you enough time to ask Gabby out again?"

Agatha hopped off Brandon's lap when she heard the word "walk." Brittany stood and, without waiting for an answer, grabbed the leash from the hook and snapped it on Agatha's collar.

I watched them walk out the door instead of looking at Brandon. I didn't want to make him, or let's be real here, me, feel more uncomfortable.

I took a deep breath and turned to face him. "Is that why you came?"

"Yes," he said.

"No Parisian restaurant. Just The Tasty Burger is perfect. And yes."

He smiled and stood. "Tonight too soon?"

"Nope. It is time for Brittany to stop hovering. I'll be happy to get out of the house."

"How about five-thirty?"

"Perfect."

"I'll pick you up here."

Brittany shoved her head in the door. "Finally. Can I come back in?"

"Not until you give Agatha her full twenty-minute walk," I said.

"Miranda, come and sit with Gabby," she yelled.

Miranda slipped in. She must have been spying with Brittany from the front porch. She held her hands up when Brandon passed her. "I didn't bring any wine."

———

Brandon and I entered The Tasty Burger at five forty and took a small booth in the corner.

"This is more like it," I glanced down at my favorite plaid pants. Although Miranda had offered, I hadn't let her "glam me up." I was fine being plain old Gabby Keats. Hopefully, Brandon felt the same. I had, however, allowed her to style my hair with some spiral curls and add some pink gloss on my lips.

"You mean the restaurant?" He looked around at the retro design, complete with a jukebox and yellow plastic-covered booths.

"Yes, that too."

"Yes, it suits you. And as much as I liked your outfit on our last date, I like seeing you being, well … you."

I didn't get a chance to answer because a much-changed, cleaned-up version of Owen stopped by our table with Tammy by his side.

Owen slid into the booth next to Brandon, and Tammy slid in on my side. "I just wanted to thank you,

Gabby, for believing in me," Owen said. Gone was the battered briefcase and ragged army surplus jacket. Instead, he wore a suit jacket, crisp white button down, and dark jeans. It was almost as if... no it couldn't be. Was that James's spicy brand of cologne I detected?

"I want to thank you for talking some sense into him," Tammy said, turning toward me in the booth and giving me a quick hug.

"Well, we'll let you two enjoy your dinner," Tammy added. She stood and gave Owen a quick side nod, indicating he should stand.

As he linked arms with Tammy, he turned and added, "James is going to help me write my first mystery novel."

I knew it. He was wearing James's signature cologne. I noticed he didn't say "bestseller." Maybe he was free of his dad's controlling you-have-to-be-the-best mindset.

"That's such good news," I said. "I can't wait to read it."

They left and I turned back to Brandon, who was studying me with a curious gaze of admiration. "The people of Maplewood look to you for advice. They respect you."

"Thank you for noticing. Wasn't it you who said 'And Gabby, don't you and The Sleuths try to solve a crime that doesn't exist'?"

"That's when I was new in town." He held his hand over his heart in mock horror.

"That was last week, when I wrote the Agatha Christie Copycat Killer Article," Brittany said from behind me.

"That's true," I agreed.

"I guess I was wrong."

"Finally," Antonio shouted from the doorway. "The engagement party." I had a perfect view of the doorway. James, Randolph, Emory, Thomas and Simone – with linked arms to boot — followed Antonio in.

My face felt as if someone had stuck it in the french fryer. "I'm never going to live that down."

"I brought you a present," Antonio said as he waddled over to our booth. "A gift certificate for a free pizza, no. Go on a date. Alone."

"I thought this was a date," I whispered to Brandon.

Honestly, solving a murder had been less complicated than trying to have one quiet dinner in Maplewood.

"It is," Brittany said as she rounded the table. "Scoot over, Gabby."

"Are we ever going to be alone?" Brandon whispered.

"I guess not until you get married, my dear boy." James scooted onto the bench next to him while the rest of The Sleuths grabbed chairs and scooted them over to our table.

"The happy couple is getting married," Antonio shouted. "Give us a bottle of something to celebrate."

"Not for you," Brittany commanded as the waitress brought a cheap burger joint bottle of wine over along with glasses.

I took a glass. "Why not? I already proposed."

She jerked it out of my hand.

"I'm kidding. I'll take some iced tea."

Brandon laughed. "I didn't say yes."

"Oh but my dear boy, you didn't say no." James smacked him on the back.

Brandon looked as if he had swallowed the cork. He coughed and looked at me. "No, I didn't say no."

———

What to read next -Fatal Footnote: A Bookstore Cozy Mystery of Murder, Mayhem, and Manuscripts (Maplewood Mysteries Book 2)

NOTES

1. THE BOOK CLUB

1. Agatha Christie, *A Murder Is Announced*
2. Agatha Christie, *A Murder Is Announced*

4. THE SLEUTHS

1. Agatha Christie, *A Caribbean Mystery*

5. MISS MARPLE

1. Agatha Christie, *The Body in The Library*
2. Agatha Christie, *The Complete Miss Marple Collection*

8. THE AGATHA CHRISTIE COPYCAT KILLER

1. Agatha Christie, *The Murder at the Vicarage*

10. A COFFEE BRIBE AND A SIDE OF BETRAYAL

1. Agatha Christie, *The Murder at the Vicarage*

12. SUSPECT SPOTLIGHT

1. Agatha Christie, *Sleeping Murder*

ABOUT THE AUTHOR

Kathleen Guire is the mother of seven, four through adoption, NiNi of fifteen, former National Parent of the Year, author, teacher, and speaker. She loves connecting with readers through her website (Kathleenguireau thor.com).

For more information,
about Kathleen, check out her website and follow her
on social media!
www.kathleenguireauthor.com
kathleenguire@gmail.com
https://linktr.ee/kguire